ANNA
AT THE MANOR HOUSE

ANNA
AT THE
MANOR HOUSE

Martha Sandwall-Bergström
Translated by Joan Tate

BLACKIE

ISBN 0 216 90771 3

Blackie & Son Ltd.,
A Member of the Blackie Group
Furnival House
14/18 High Holborn
London WC1

Printed in Great Britain by
The Anchor Press Ltd
Tiptree, Essex

One

Every morning, the children came trooping down the main staircase in a nervous, orderly line, tidily dressed, their hair plastered down with water, their cheeks glowing from the thorough treatment they had received from soap, water and towel. They curtseyed and bowed, shifting their feet and staring.

"Good morning, sir," said John, bowing so low and humbly that his fiery red hair flopped over his nose, his forehead almost touching his knees.

"Good morning," whispered the twins, Willie and Vera. They were clutching hands, their eyes round and anxious below their fair fringes. They curtseyed and bowed, bowed and curtseyed, always forgetting which should do which.

"Good morning, good morning," cried Addie in a loud voice, because the more nervous he was, the more confident he tried to sound. He also bowed several times, his fat cheeks wobbling.

"Mornin', mornin'," piped Sofia, giving a little bob, then another, her quick squirrel-brown eyes darting round, taking in as much as possible. She curtseyed to the Patron, to the stuffed elk-head on the wall, and to the bearskin on the floor. "Mornin', mornin', everybody." Then she curtseyed to the tall clock in the corner, which at that moment said five minutes to seven. Then to the funny "tellyfon". A little troll lived inside its black stomach and answered in a strange voice far away when you wound the handle and lifted the receiver. Sofia had several times heard the Patron talking to the troll. "Mornin', mornin'." It was best to be just as polite to the one as to the other.

Mr Sylvester was sitting by the fire, taking his morning coffee. He turned slowly towards the bunch of children standing by the doorway. They were forbidden to step over the threshold. The firelight fell on him, giving a little colour to his face, his grey hair, grey moustache and bushy grey eyebrows. It also shone on the porcelain and silver on the tray, on his well-polished boots and the monocle he had raised to his eye. In silence, he looked them over sternly for a few seconds before replying.

"Good morning, children," he said.

The morning inspection was over without comment or correction. The children heaved a sigh of relief, huddled together even more closely and let Anna through. She always stayed behind them, like a small mother-hen shooing her chicks ahead of her.

"Good morning, Grandfather," she said, smiling and stepping into the room, as no thresholds hindered her way. Neither was she as nervous and scared as the others, for she was the child of the house. Although she held the grey-haired old man in great respect, she also felt tenderness and love for him. She went over and kissed him on the cheek. Her eyes were shining and clear, a serious deep-blue smile in their depths. Her hair was damp from her morning toilet, curling in fair ringlets round her forehead and temples. She held out her strong little girl's hand, and each morning the children were able to watch the miracle of the old man's stern clouded face dissolving into a smile that was happy and almost tender.

"Good morning, my child," he said, his voice a thousand times more friendly than when he had said "Good morning, children".

That was as it should be, the children thought, and none was envious. They knew that they were allowed to live at the manor only because of Anna, and the kinder he was towards Anna, the safer they felt. None of the five crofter children had yet overcome their terror of being on the parish or of the poor-house, their terror of loneliness and beatings and hunger. Their gratitude to the Patron, who had allowed them to stay with Anna, was boundless, but combined with constant anxiety that they would not live up to expectations. They bowed and curtseyed and shifted their feet whenever he came within sight. They held their breath when he spoke, staring wide-eyed and expectant, waiting for a brightening of his usually grim features.

But he seldom had a personal word or a kindly smile for any of them. His hostility towards the poor was deep-rooted, and that he tolerated having the children of one of his own crofters living with him was something that surprised even himself. He thought they were impossible. Their awkwardness, their staring eyes and anxiously gaping mouths and their clumsy behaviour all offended him. They had none of the inborn charm, none of the natural grace and dignity that made Anna the attractive child she was. He had been captivated by her from the very first moment, before he had even known who she was. There was a nobility of breeding in her. She was affectionate and pleasant, although she had had no fine upbringing. The Patron liked showing her off to friends and guests.

"This is my grand-daughter, Annemaria Beatrice Frederika, my daughter's daughter, by a miracle discovered again," he used to say.

Then he would make her stand by the picture in the drawing-room so that they could marvel at the likeness to the dead Annemaria Beatrice, whose fair curls, strangely slanting eyes and heart-shaped face were so precisely repeated in her living namesake. The Patron felt then that the clock had turned back and he now had both his daughter and grand-daughter with him in the same person: Annemaria Beatrice Frederika, in a miraculous way, found again.

But these five poor crofter's brats had given his home the air of a charitable institution. From the start, he had given orders that they were not to trouble him, not to run about the house, not to slam the doors, not to make a noise in the rooms, and yet to him they still seemed to be in his way and they irritated him. He had had them clothed from head to foot in new garments, but although he was sure they were bathed and clean—Mademoiselle Modig was not one to be careless in such details—the all-pervading smell of the crofter's cottage seemed to surround them. Sometimes he was embarrassed over what his friends and acquaintances might think or say.

"But they must be allowed to stay for the time being," he said to himself, remembering the day Anna had come driving home with the whole flock of them in the sleigh. "I let myself be persuaded and promised them a home. Anna trusts me to keep my word."

The breakfast bell rang out from one of the gables. Foreman Germaine, always called the German because of his strange name, the dark stubble on his chin and his foreign looks, was standing pulling the rope. Ding-dong, ding-dong. The peals rang out that it was now seven o'clock and time for porridge for the farm-men who had already been at work for two or three hours. From the fields, where spring cultivation had begun, from barns and sheds, the labourers came clumping in their clogs to the manor house kitchen. There the maidservants, hot from the stove, hurriedly poured the porridge out of the pan. The children would be waiting for their food in the pantry beyond the kitchen, where Mademoiselle had arranged a table for them. When they had bowed and curtseyed once again to the Patron, they trooped out. Sofia furtively tried to stick her foot over the forbidden threshold of the study, just to feel if the floor there really was as slippery as it looked. But she was dragged hastily back by her terrified brothers and sisters.

"Haven't you got no sense?" they whispered, holding firmly on to her dress as they pattered across the hall and out into the pantry, Anna following them. Although she ate her other meals in the dining-room with the Patron, she had pleaded with him to be allowed at least once a day to help them at table.

"They're so clumsy and nervous still, Grandfather dear. They feel safe if I'm with them," she had said. In the end, the Patron had given in, although he disliked sitting alone at breakfast while Anna was dispensing kindness at the other end of the house.

"It's strange, what's happened to the Patron," Mademoiselle said after overhearing this conversation. "He was so stern and strict with his own daughter, and now he can't have enough of his grand-daughter. It's as if he'd discovered he'd been living in a desert all his life, and now suddenly couldn't get enough water."

"Yes," said Anna, thoughtfully. She saw her grandfather's heart as a thirsty wilting plant, aching for the water of love. She was eager to give as much as she could from her own overflowing heart. But she found it confusing that he did not understand that she had to have time for the children. They were small plants, too, needing her care and attention. The days when the Patron quite selfishly took up her time were difficult. She did not enjoy sitting by the fire in the study, playing chess or dominoes, while the children stood staring longingly through the crack in the door. And the delicious food served in the dining-room did not taste so good when she knew the children out in the pantry were not receiving the same. When she was told to put on her best dress, let her hair down in ringlets and come to the drawing-room where there were guests, she did so without pleasure, for on such occasions the children were told to keep away and not be a nuisance. When she was finally released and had a moment to devote to them, they ran to her with the same hunger in their eyes as when she used to return from her duties at the manor with perhaps a little bread to share among them.

"We've been waiting *so* long, Anna," they would say, as the younger ones clambered all over her, stroking her soft velvet dress, unable to get close enough. "We've been waiting and *waiting*, Anna, all day, for hours and hours and *hours*."

As Anna stood there with the clinging, pushing flock all round her, she realised there was a hunger other than the hunger for food that needed to be stilled. She had managed to get them good warm clothes, healthy food and a roof over their heads, but that was not enough for a small human being to live on. Slowly but surely, Anna realised that her difficulties had not yet been overcome, that she still had a long way to go before she could fulfil the task she had undertaken. She could not yet rest and preen herself as a well-brought-up young lady. There were many more obstacles to overcome and goals to aim for.

Two

But now they were sitting at the breakfast table with plates of porridge in front of them. They were to eat and be grateful for the good and plentiful food, for the rich porridge and the bread-and-butter and salt herring served with it. The twins sat either side of John, so that they would not squabble over the same bit of bread or herring, as they always used to, and Sofia and Addie sat beside Anna, so that she could help them if necessary.

"The food's gooder when you is with us, Anna," said Addie, spooning porridge into a mouth already full of bread and herring. Addie was six, and although the more plentiful food of the manor had already made him fatter than ever, he was nevertheless always hungry. As soon as possible, he would join the labourers in the stables and barn, preferably the stables. He helped water the horses and groom them and muck them out. Sometimes he was given a pair of reins to hold and that made him beside himself with delight. His greatest dream was to become a coachman and drive the Patron's horses.

"So the food ain't good enough otherwise, ain't it then?"

said Agda, one of the maidservants, as she came in to refill the porridge bowl. She was the servant-girl who had once pulled Anna's pigtail when she had found her gazing at the picture of Annemaria Beatrice during working hours. Agda had hardly changed since then, and of all the maidservants, she was the one who found it most difficult to forget that Anna had once been a servant in the house. She glanced indignantly at Addie.

"Perhaps he'd best stop eating at other meals, then, if they doesn't taste so good," she said, slamming the tureen down on the table with such force that the contents slopped out. Anna looked at her seriously.

"The food's always good, but what's good can taste different at different times," she said. "If you're happy, everything tastes better than when you're not. That's what he meant."

"Yes, that's just what I did meant," said Addie, pleased with her help, and chewing away even more vigorously.

"Soffytina meant that, too," said Sofia. Her names were Sofia Katrina, but so far Soffytina was as much as she could manage. She was two and a half now, and very different from her brothers and sisters in both appearance and temperament. She was small and thin and quick as a weasel, while the others were sturdy and slow in their movements. She had a narrow little face with a pointed chin, while the others had square faces. She had quick brown eyes, constrasting with the slow blue of the others. Her hair was red, not the fiery red of John's, but darker, as coarse as horsehair and dead straight. Every morning, on Mademoiselle's orders, it was plaited into four small pigtails, because it was still too short for the one or two most girls had, and Mademoiselle considered it looked untidy hanging round her face. But as soon as she could, Sofia loosened at least the front two and tried to bend the strands into curls like Anna's. She was at the imitating age and she wanted to do just what Anna did, thought or said.

"Soffytina always means what Anna means," she repeated, looking so self-important and know-all that the twins retaliated.

"You're too small to mean anything," they said.

Anna rapped on the table.

"Eat now, children," she said. "And be quiet."

"Yes, eat and be quiet," Sofia repeated at once, banging her spoon on her porridge plate.

They could hear the men's deep voices out in the kitchen and then the maids giggling and laughing at some witticism. Spoons rattled against plates, and the Patron's hound, Pompi, also came slinking in for a bowl of porridge. He growled suspiciously as he walked through the kitchen, as he was not yet used to Foreman Germaine, who was new to the estate. But when the foreman rose from the table, scraping his chair back along the floor, Pompi was frightened. With his tail between his legs, he slipped into the pantry, where he stood peering through the crack in the door. The children laughed at him.

"Looks like he's scared of getting a beating," they said, finding the idea very funny, for they knew how strict the Patron was. No one was allowed to touch his hound, either to pat him or hit him.

Then they heard a puffing and panting in the kitchen that was Mademoiselle Modig coming in from the brewhouse, where she had put two of the crofters' wives to work sterilising feathers for bolsters and pillows. A fire was lit under the great boiler to steam the sacks of feathers they collected during the winter from all the chickens and game. This was to make the feathers light and porous. But the flying dust irritated the lungs and gave the person a sore throat, so it was not a pleasant job. Mademoiselle was coughing and spluttering out in the kitchen, trying to clear her throat to speak.

"Who was last in the store-house?" she said to the maids. Despite the early hour and the fact that her bad foot made walking difficult for her, Mademoiselle had already been out on her tour of inspection of the food-stores and cellars.

"Agda, probably, I reckon. She bin to fetch a jar of mashed turnip yesterday," said one of the maids sullenly, wondering what was wrong.

Mademoiselle did not reply, but she was looking thoughtful and put out, because she hadn't known that herself. Her memory had begun to betray her recently. Although she herself thought there had been seven large pork sausages hanging out there in the store-house, she could not swear to it. Anyhow, there were only five now. She didn't wish to call anyone a thief if he was not one, so she said nothing, sighing a little over her poor memory, and limping in to the children at their breakfast.

"Good morning, children," she said, trying to look strict. She thought that children, especially poor children who were suddenly better off, should be treated strictly so that they did not become spoilt. But she was careful not to be as hard and cruel as the Patron had been many a time in his younger days, when his daughter was still alive. Strictness was another matter, however, and Mademoiselle tried to conjure some up, although it was difficult for her. She had always loved children, and she enjoyed having them in the house.

The children all got up and greeted her politely as she came in. "Good morning, good morning," they said, looking happy, because they knew they had a friend in Mademoiselle Modig.

17

They willingly submitted themselves to her inspection as she limped round the table, looking into their ears and at their necks, making sure they had washed properly. Sofia was scolded for already having one of her ribbons undone, but only mildly, because in Mademoiselle's heart of hearts, Sofia was her favourite.

"Leave your plaits alone, or it'll be a smack for you," she warned, tying up the ribbon and patting the child on the head.

"Want to be like Anna," said Sofia, pulling the ribbon undone again.

"I'll go upstairs and plait my hair, then we'll be the same," said Anna, laughing and tying up the ribbon again.

"Do that," said Mademoiselle, to avoid having to smack the child, for Sofia was now untying the ribbon for the third time.

"Want to be like Anna," she said firmly.

After breakfast, John and the twins went off to school, after Anna had hurriedly heard their homework for a last time. John was twelve now and in the top grade. The twins were eight and in the first grade. They should have started school the previous year, but they had been lodged out by the parish. When the crofter at Svenne Croft had wanted work out of them in exchange for their keep, the parish had made no objections. The crofters thought children should first learn to work, so that they could earn their keep. Learning to read, write and do sums was all very well, but a luxury for a poor man.

John was doing much better at school than before, and Mr Bromander had never once had to beat him with his cane. Once or twice, Mr Bromander had even felt driven to praise him. This was indeed very strange for John, the crooked-backed dunce of before, always bottom of the class, and deaf too, so that he had to lipread to understand what people said. Mr Bromander praised him and said that some kind of blockage must have suddenly melted away, making it possible for him to learn. John quietly accepted the words of praise, smiling slightly, because he knew the blockage had not been inside him, but outside. Now that he no longer had to strain his thin body with inhuman work, now that day after day he no longer had to saw logs, drive charcoal-carts, and heave flour-sacks at a grown man's pace, he had both strength and time for homework. Now homework had become a pleasant task and even fun instead of a torment. John read and studied and asked Anna to hear him and explain, and what he lacked in talent, he made up for in perseverance and industry.

Three

Anna would very much have liked to go with them to school. Over the years her attendance there had been spasmodic and dependent on the time her masters and employers reckoned they could spare her. But she was fourteen now and the Patron did not want to see her sitting among the farmers' children in the parish school. He had decided that she should have a rest after all she had been through during the spring and summer. Then in the autumn she would go to a good girls' boarding school, where they would give her an education that was in keeping with her station.

Until then, the Patron taught her a little each day, mostly things that amused him. He gave her books from his shelves and urged her to read Dickens and Walter Scott and Homer and many many more. Anna took the books up to her room and read them there with John. A whole new vista of worlds they had never even imagined before now opened out in front of the two children's eyes.

But the Patron usually wanted Anna with him in his study in the daytime, as he was still weak from the severe bout of typhoid fever he had only just got over. She helped him add up columns of figures as he went through his accounts. He liked her reading aloud to him, as well as playing chess or dominoes with him. He often took her with him into his office. Every morning after breakfast and every evening before their meal, he received his foreman, his steward and crofters, to find out how the work was going and settle necessary accounts.

"There's no harm in you seeing how things work," he said. "In a few years' time you'll be grown up, and I'll perhaps be gone and will have left the responsibility to you."

"Yes," said Anna, uneasily, sitting at the little desk, trying to make herself useful by adding figures and tidying papers as she watched the men shuffling in and bowing, submissive before the Patron. Sometimes it was the steward of the estate come to complain about deliveries of charcoal from one of the crofters. Sometimes it was the foreman, Germaine hurrying in to say that one of the beasts was sick, and to discuss whether the vet from town should be sent for or whether Wise Manda would do. Sometimes he was there complaining about the insolence and laziness of the labourers. And sometimes the labourers came themselves in a dark mumbling bunch, complaining about the foreman. Perman, the old coachman, came stumping in, his goatee beard whipping, complaining that the fodder rations for his horses were too small. Sometimes a starving crofter came begging in the name of mercy for half a bag of rye on credit from the Patron.

Sometimes the men left calmed and helped, but sometimes it was the other way round, their faces even more troubled, their eyes dark, their backs bowed in despair, for the Patron was a harsh master, demanding a great deal and seldom giving anything freely. Everyone said that he had grown milder in his old age, but as he sat there behind his great oak desk, clutching the long ruler that before he had never hesitated to use as a weapon, he was still an authoritative and frighteningly powerful figure.

That morning when Anna went to the office with him, the foreman was waiting outside the closed door, one hand grasping the collar of a labourer's boy hardly older than Anna herself, deathly white and trembling in the face of what was to come.

"Here's the egg-thief!" said Germaine triumphantly. He took a firmer grasp on the boy's collar, as if afraid the wretch would escape, although the boy was shaking like a leaf and hardly able to stand upright. "Caught him in the act, I did."

The Patron looked reluctantly at the boy. He was ragged and thin, unkempt and dirty. He was the son of a forest cottager by the name of Kari, who at one time had spun the flax that the maidservants couldn't manage. Kari was ill now and the boy, Mats, had been given a job as labourer's boy at the manor as an act of charity.

The Patron looked away and opened the door to the office. "Come in," he said, walking round and sitting down at the desk. The foreman followed him in, triumphantly dragging the boy with him.

For several weeks, Germaine said, it had been clear that eggs were disappearing from the hen-house, not many at a time, oh, no, a careful thief. It was not impossible, he said, that the labourers and the milking-maids occasionally stole an egg, pricking a hole in it and sucking it quickly, because they dared not hide it in their clothes—indeed, he kept a careful check and examined every pocket that bulged suspiciously. Oh, no, Mr

Sylvester, he certainly did not neglect his duties, however unpleasant it might be to have the servants against him. Oh, no, he knew only too well what his employer demanded of his foreman. Well, the theft of eggs had gone on, although he personally had supervised the maids in the hen-house and then padlocked the door himself, so that no one could get in until feeding-time the next day. And today, when he had happened to go to the barn an hour or two earlier than usual—well, not quite by chance, but in the course of duty, as he had been worried about a calving cow—he had heard something scratching in the hen-house, and this boy had come wriggling through the opening the hens used for going in and out. If he'd given it any thought, he would have realised that the thief must have been as small and thin as this boy. But he didn't want to think it was him, to whom the Patron had in his mercy given work and food, and who had now rewarded his master so ill. But then people had no shame today, you know, Mr Sylvester, you should just see how the men behave these days. . . .

"That'll do, Germaine!" The Patron held up his hand to stop his loquacious foreman, and turned to the boy standing there, quietly sobbing in Germaine's firm grip.

"Do you admit to stealing eggs from the hen-house?"

"Yes," whimpered the boy, wild-eyed with fear, white in the face.

The Patron looked sternly at him.

"Didn't you learn the Ten Commandments at school? Thou shalt not steal, one of them says. Do you know it?"

"Yes," said the boy, tearfully.

"Then you should remember it and keep it in mind," said the Patron "Hold out your hands."

"No, no!" cried the boy, looking as if he might faint. Over by the door, Anna looked pleadingly at the Patron.

"Grandfather, dear . . ."

"Be quiet," said the Patron, indignant now, the scene distasteful to him.

"Hold out your hands," he said again, "and let's get this over and done with. Come on, boy!"

But the boy refused until Germaine forced him to do what the Patron had ordered. With the heavy ruler, the Patron struck seven stinging blows on those thin dirty hands. Seven strokes to remind him of the Seventh Commandment. Broad red weals rose on the skin.

"Never forget the Seventh Commandment again," said the Patron.

The boy had stopped crying as the blows started raining down on his hands, but then something terrible happened. He suddenly leant forward and spat straight in the Patron's face.

The two men were aghast. Neither of them had ever experienced anything like it. A labourer spitting at the Patron —spitting straight in his face? No, that was impossible. They stared as if they could not believe their eyes. The Patron fell back against the back of the chair, as if he needed support to be able to wonder whether all this had really happened. The spit ran down his face and his mouth fell open. For a moment, he looked no more intelligent than his gaping foreman.

The boy took the opportunity. With a jerk, he tore himself free and headed for the door. Fumbling with the handle for a moment, he then opened it, glancing back with the look of a wild animal.

"Our cow's dead, and Mum's ill!" he shouted. "And we

needs eggs more than you!" Then he spat again and vanished.

Germaine at last pulled himself together, and with a bellow of rage, he rushed out after the boy. The Patron straightened up in his chair, got out his handkerchief with a trembling hand and wiped the spit away. His face was grey.

"You go on out," he said to Anna, who was still standing by the door. He seemed to be angry with her for having seen what had happened.

Anna went out and sat down on the stairs in the hall. Her knees were weak and she felt sick. She didn't really know what was the matter with her. She was used to beatings, both receiving them herself and seeing others receive them. Beatings were unpleasant, but quite usual, part of being a child and not yet grown up. You were beaten if you did something bad or silly, sometimes even when it was not your fault, according to the whims of adults. You had to endure it and think about it affecting only your skin. It soon passed and then you were happy again.

But what she had witnessed today upset her in a way that neither Karlberg striking the children at home at Kulla, nor the miller beating John had ever done. Then she had been cross and indignant and had acted accordingly. But now it seemed like a pain inside her and she didn't know what to do. When John took a beating, he did so in a humble and submissive way, and although he cried and was afraid, he was soon consoled. And never, however badly he had been treated, never had she seen in his eyes what she had seen in Mats's.

She sat there for a long time thinking about those eyes. In the end she knew what she had seen—it was hatred, the hatred felt by one who is desperate and defenceless, but who neither understands that with calm one can overcome it, as she herself had learnt, nor has the strength to forgive, as John had.

"Some people are made in one way, some in another," she thought.

Four

The incident between the Patron and the young thief was now on everyone's tongue, because Germaine had gone round shouting to the men to go and find Mats, who had disappeared on his spindly legs into the forest like a hunted elk-calf. The men obeyed and went off in search of the boy, at heart reluctant, more on the boy's side than the foreman's. So as soon as they were out of sight of the farm buildings, they sat down for a pinch of snuff and a chat, then turned back saying that they hadn't been able to find Mats. Germaine shouted and swore with rage, saying the boy had to be punished for his shameless behaviour. The maids in the kitchen whispered and shook their heads, and the crofters' wives working at the feather-cleaning came out and stood on the steps, listening, pale and silent, to the foreman's rage. The Patron had shut himself in his office, refusing to show himself, as was his habit when he was very annoyed and hurt about something. Anna dared not go in to him. Instead, she crept away to find Mademoiselle, as she wanted permission to go up to Kari with a basket of food.

"Then perhaps I could talk to Mats at the same time," she thought, trying to think of a way out for him.

Mademoiselle was just about to go out, and she asked Anna to take pen and paper and come with her, because she was going to do her rounds of the store-houses, lofts and cellars, to make an inventory. She would have to keep written accounts of the food-stores now, she said, as her memory was going and she could not keep the numbers of hams, sausages or butter-pats in her head. She was quite worried about the present situation out there. She had an idea that two sausages were missing.

"Supposing the boy's been there, too?" she said, looking scared.

They went out after Mademoiselle had made Anna put on two cardigans, gaiters and her fur cap. No matter how much Anna protested, Mademoiselle refused to remember that for months on end Anna had walked barefoot on frosty ground and worn no more clothes than were absolutely necessary to keep her warm. Now that Anna had become a young lady, in Mademoiselle's eyes, she was a delicate, vulnerable object.

The store was long and narrow, with small windows high up. The walls were lined with shelves of ripening cheeses of different sizes, and long rows of fat stoneware jars of preserves. On the floor were bins of flour and oats, peas, brown beans and dried fruit. There were great vats of salt-pork and meat, barrels of butter, gherkins and runner beans, and hanging from the ceiling were rows of sausages, hams and dried legs of lamb on large hooks. Barrels of salt herring there were, too, and a couple of kegs of syrup. The smells of the different foodstuffs made the air heavy and spice-laden.

Mademoiselle limped inside and sat down on a keg, puffing a little, because she had difficulty walking with her bad foot, so she was putting on weight fast. Her body was now so heavy that she became breathless and sweaty at the slightest exertion.

"Poof!" she said, wiping her forehead with her spotless white linen handkerchief, and rubbing her bad foot, which was always swollen. Nowadays she could not get a shoe on to it. She was wearing the large slipper she always wore indoors, and out-of-doors she wore one of the Patron's discarded galoshes on top.

After resting for a few minutes, she brightened and started. She inspected the rows of jars like a general inspecting his troops. She counted the cheeses, the hams and the legs of lamb, calling out the numbers to Anna, who wrote them down. When it came to counting the sausages, Mademoiselle let out a cry of alarm. She could not make them more than one hundred and twenty-six. And yet that morning when she had gone out to fetch two for the Patron's breakfast, she had counted them over quickly and made a hundred and thirty-six. What had happened?

"You must have counted wrong," said Anna, standing there with her notebook, oppressed by the over-abundance of food, and thinking of Mats. His hands, thin and knobbly like a fully grown man's, but with wrists even thinner and weaker than John's—they were still in her mind as they were held out to receive punishment. Now they seemed to be stretching out towards the abundance in the food-store.

"Please, Mademoiselle, let me take a basket of food up to Kari," she said quickly, thinking it would be best to ask now before Mademoiselle went on with her inventory and perhaps found more things missing.

But Mademoiselle turned round looking extremely displeased.

"Certainly not," she said.

"But Kari's been ill for so long, perhaps they haven't got anything to eat," said Anna.

"Her son seems to have arranged all right for what they have," said Mademoiselle, turning back to the sausages. "If we give them something now, it would almost be like rewarding him for thieving."

"But if there was food in the cottage, there wouldn't be any need for him to steal," said Anna. "Perhaps with a basket of food now and again, we could save him from the sin and shame." She looked hopefully at Mademoiselle standing there looking up at the hundred and twenty-six sausages and counting. Anna knew Mademoiselle and knew that it was worth asking. For although Mademoiselle was extremely careful and economical with the bounties at her disposal through her service with the Patron, and although she was outwardly strict and firm, she had a good heart and was kindly towards everything poor and helpless. But she did not wish to show it, and she was also anxious about what the Patron would say.

"I'll talk to Grandfather about it myself," said Anna, to meet Mademoiselle on that point, too.

"You'd better wait until afterwards," said Mademoiselle, reluctantly taking down some sausages and handing them with an unwilling expression to Anna. "You're no better than your mother was in her time," she scolded. "And I suppose you'll never give in until you get your own way. Take these sausages, and the smallest cheese on the shelf, that butter-pat there, and a piece of pork out of the vat. Then go to the milk-shed for a little milk and fetch some loaves from the loft. Then off you go to Kari while it's still light. I can't have you running about in the forest after dark."

"Thank you so much," said Anna radiantly, curtseying. "Don't you want me to stay and write things down any more, then?"

"Oh, I can do that," said Mademoiselle. "Run along now, before it gets dark. And remember that the Patron will not be pleased when he hears about it."

"No," said Anna, sighing slightly. "But that can't be helped, can it?"

"No, it probably can't," said Mademoiselle, sighing, too. At the door, she called Anna back.

"Take a little cream and a batch of eggs while you're at it," she said. "I mean, now that you're going all that way."

"Oh, thank you," said Anna.

She ran into the kitchen for a basket and in the yard she came across Sofia jumping round the puddles, pretending that she was the hound, Pompi.

"Bow-wow!" she said, flinging back her plaits and jumping up and down. "Bow-wow-wow." She rushed at the flagpole—that was the foreman—barking wildly. "Bow-wow-wow!"

Agda came across from the barn with a shoulder-yoke, and the child began barking at her, too.

"Bow-wow!" she said, growling down in her throat, then backing away just like a dog. "Bow-wow."

But Agda was not amused. She smacked Sofia across the bottom with the yoke.

"Behave yourself," she said crossly. Then she hit out with the yoke again, because Sofia was rushing after her, trying to bite her. Anna ran forward before anything could happen and took Sofia by the hand.

"Come on, and we'll go and pack this basket with food," she said. "Come on, now, you can help me pack the basket."

"Pack food, pack food," said Sofia, at once forgetting her fury. "Help pack food. Soffytina help Anna."

But Agda went into the kitchen in a very bad temper.

"I suppose she's going to give food to some cottager again now," she said to the other maids. "Pork and sausages and preserves and butter again, all given away to people what doesn't bother to do nothing but sit at home. And if I what works and slaves away day in and day out as much as sniffed at the end of a sausage or put my little finger in the syrup keg, oh, what a hullaballoo there'd be then."

Anna went out to the store again and took down the things she'd been promised for Mats's sick mother. Sofia went with her, scuttling round the barrels and flour-bins with interest. She kept asking Mademoiselle for a little syrup.

"Syrwup," she cried, looking coy and sweet. "Syrwup, syrwup. Syrwup, please."

"Certainly not," said Mademoiselle, looking stern. In the end, Sofia grew tired and went off, and Mademoiselle's expression softened as she watched her go.

"Like a baby squirrel," she said, and after struggling inwardly for a few seconds, she went over to a cupboard on the short wall and unlocked it. That was where they kept the sugar hidden from greedy eyes, fine pure white caster sugar that appeared only on the Patron's table, while the rest had to make do with syrup and loaf-sugar wrapped in brown paper. Mademoiselle took up her little sugar tongs that, together with her scissors and the bunch of keys, always hung by her apron, and cut off two sizeable pieces of sugar.

"You give these to the little ones," she said. "Because I don't want to be the one to spoil them."

Anna hurried away as soon as she had packed the basket.

She was eager to be home again before the Patron asked for her. Sofia and Addie were out by the stables. She shared the largest lump of sugar between them and told them to be good while she was out. They promised faithfully. Sofia dug her sharp little teeth into the sugar and crunched it up, her quick brown eyes alight with pleasure. Addie looked equally delighted, but he sucked very carefully round the edge of his lump. He was going to save a bit for Clio, a black foal in a box inside the stables, his greatest love among the horses.

They went up towards the forest with her for a while and then stood waving to her.

"Hurry on back, Anna, won't you?" they said. Like their brothers and sisters, they were always anxious when they knew Anna was out of reach.

Five

Kari's home was on the other side of the forest, far beyond both Kulla and Backen Crofts and Dally-Peter's cottage. It was not one of the estate's, but on a great heath called the Common, where the crofters grazed their sheep in summer. The red colour of the cottage had darkened over the years and was now as brown as the heather on the heath. The roof was brown too, as it was made of turf, and against all this brown, the chimney stood out white like a piece of sugar. At a distance, it was just like the cottage in the story of Hansel and Gretel.

But once you were over the threshold, the likeness immediately vanished. It was poor and shabby inside, the floor of stamped earth and the door into the room so crooked and warped that it squealed like a stuck pig when it was opened. The walls smelt musty with damp and ingrained cooking smells.

Anna stood by the door, blinking in the half-light after the clear light of the heath outside, hardly able to distinguish a thing.

"Good day, Mother Kari," she said to the person she knew

to be there. A weak voice came from the far corner of the room and when Anna's eyes had got used to the dim light, she saw that Kari was lying on a wooden sofa by the stove. She went over and greeted her, taking her hand. But she had to pick up the sick woman's hand from the covers, as Mother Kari could not lift it. Her face was white and sunken against the end of the sofa.

"Who . . . who is it?" she said.

"I'm from the manor," said Anna, curtseying. "Mademoiselle has sent up a basket of things and asks how you are."

She began unpacking the basket and placing the contents on the table, so that Mother Kari could see. The sick woman shook her head.

"Oh, how good of Mademoiselle! She's too kind, that she is. That'll be good for my boy when he comes home. Oh, how good."

"You must eat some yourself, too, Mother Kari," said Anna. Then she asked if it would be all right if she arranged a plateful, as she realised the sick woman could not even get out of bed. Presumably Mats did all the work when he came back in the evenings.

But Mother Kari went on shaking her head. Oh, no, she could not eat much. There was no point, because she always brought it up again, however hungry she was, and that was such a waste, a sinful waste of God's gifts. She hadn't been able to keep anything down for a long time except a yolk of egg or two that Mats mixed with a little milk. If she took a spoonful at a time of that mixture and waited a while between each spoonful, she managed to keep it down.

"So thank Mademoiselle ever so much for sending them eggs with Mats nearly every week, won't you? So kind of her, when there ain't nothing left in a poor person's store. Just a few turnips in the stack outside, that's all we've left, and we've only those because the cow, our poor old cow, was found dead in its stall one morning in the winter. Oh, what a misfortune that was, oh, dear, oh dear. How Mats cried that morning and how I felt it, too. And so empty it's been, almost worse than when out eldest went off to America. And we'll never get another cow, now."

Mother Kari spoke in short broken sentences, panting and gasping for air between words. Beneath the wrinkled skin of her throat, a pulse was beating wildly. Then she grew so tired that she fell silent and leant against the end of the sofa again. Anna took an egg out of the basket, broke the yolk into a cup, then stirred in a little cream and gave it to her. The sick woman shook her head again and was so grateful, so grateful.

"Has Mademoiselle sent eggs today, too? Oh, so kind of her. Much too kind of her. As soon as I'm well and up and about again, I'll be spinning flax and carding wool in return for all this kindness, yes, that I promise. Mats brings a few eggs almost every week, and I'd never have got through without them when I were really bad, that I wouldn't. Though I doesn't wish to complain in any way. So please tell Mademoiselle and thank her so much for them eggs."

"Yes, I will," said Anna, realising which eggs they had been. Cautiously, she asked after Mats. Had he by any chance come home?

"No, Mats don't come home till evening. He works at the manor like a fully grown man, though he's only fourteen. He's a good boy, the last of them all. The others is all in America. I hopes Mats'll be able to stay on at the manor. It'll be good to know where he is, should it so happen that I can't get up again. You never know—today red, tomorrow dead, they say, doesn't they?"

"Yes," said Anna, looking at the sunken white face, which had certainly not had any healthy red colour in its cheeks for a long time. Then she looked round the cottage and asked if there was anything she could do. She straightened out the sick woman's bed and shook out the straw pillows, then swept the floor, beat the rag-rugs and ran down to the spring for water, despite the woman's protests, all the time expecting Mats to come home. But he didn't.

"Perhaps he's gone back to apologise and accept the punishment promised by the foreman," she thought, feeling better on his behalf. Difficult things became simpler and frightening things less frightening as long as you could bring yourself to face them.

She said goodbye to Kari, who repeated her messages of thanks to Mademoiselle. Then she went off with her empty basket. The bright light of the heath made her eyes water, and she stood for a moment on the doorstep while her eyes grew accustomed to it. Then she saw something written in the melting snowdrift by the wall of the cottage. "Tell-tale, tell-tale."

She looked at the words in bewilderment and then as she raised her head, she thought she saw someone slipping round the corner of the empty cowshed. She went across.

"Mats!" she called quietly. "Is that you, Mats?"

No one replied and there was no sign of anyone. Marks of clogs could be seen here and there in the snow, but not necessarily new ones. She stood there thinking and suddenly a hard-packed snowball hit the back of her neck. It hurt so much that her head sang. Quickly she flung the empty basket over her head to protect her from the next one.

"Mats!" she called again, keeping her voice low so that she shouldn't be heard inside the cottage. "Mats! Come out, won't you?"

But no one appeared. Neither did any more snowballs, and in the end she hadn't time to stay any longer. With the basket over her head, she went back to the snowdrift by the house, rubbed out the words there and then wrote some herself.

"Don't be afraid," she wrote. "I haven't said anything. Come down to the Patron and clear things up."

Then she put the sugar-lump she had hidden in her pocket on to the edge of the stone step with a little piece of paper underneath it. There was a small patch of snow there, too. So she wrote:

"For you. Don't be afraid."

For safety's sake, she kept the basket on her head as she hurried away home.

Six

The bell at the manor rang out for evening coffee and the men
tramped in from barn, stable and field. They were still talking
about Mats Kari, which was what the boy was usually called
to distinguish him from another Mats in the crowd of
labourer's boys, and there was amazement at the thought of
what the boy had done. Spat in the face of the Patron! They
couldn't discuss the event enough.

"The nerve of it," they said, shocked and delighted at the
same time, for anything daring, bad or good, made their
stomachs curl. Foreman Germaine, of course, stumped round
looking industrious, still indignant on behalf of the Patron.

"Tell me as soon as the boy shows his face here again," he
said, frowning heavily with his jet-black eyebrows, his face
with its dark stubble tense, his eyes hard and yellowish brown,
like a cat's. The men nodded and mumbled that they would, but
they made rude faces behind his back.

"Snotty German," they said, as they found his manner hard
to bear.

There was even more talk in the kitchen. The maids said

that Mademoiselle had come in from the stores in a bad mood. She had asked about pork and sausages and butter and who had fetched what last from there and how much had been fetched. It was as if she meant things were missing from the store. Perhaps Mats Kari had been in several places apart from the hen-house? One of the girls remembered that just before Christmas, she had lost the brooch her fiancé had given her, and that day Mats had been in for a drink of water out of the scoop. She had thought she had probably dropped the brooch, but you could never be sure when there was a thief about.

"Yes," said the other girls, and everyone remembered something that had been lost. Agda suddenly remembered that when Mademoiselle had sent her out for pork to be soaked for the next day's turnip-mash, she had thought someone was behind her. It had been evening, so she had had a lantern with her and had said, "Who's there?" Of course, no one had answered, and so she hadn't given it another thought. But if things were missing out there, then . . .

"Yes," said the others, and no one knew what to believe.

The children, sitting round the table in the pantry, heard the talk through the open door and listened with their mouths open. A thief, how terrible! They gaped and listened, their eyes wide-open. Only John, just back from school with the twins, heard nothing. He sat smiling to himself, thinking of other things.

Anna hurried through the room so quickly that she only had time to nod and smile at them, because the Patron did not like people coming late for meals. She had taken off her gaiters and outer clothes and brushed her hair and washed after her visit to Kari's cottage. Her cheeks were red and her eyes bright after the long walk back through the forest, and a whiff of fresh spring air wafted round her. Sofia grabbed her skirt.

"Sit, Anna," she demanded.

"No, poppet, I'm in a hurry to go to Grandfather," said Anna, freeing herself from the little hand. "I'll be back later."

Sofia slid off her chair, wanting to come, too.

"Soffytina in hurry to Ganfie too," she said, looking important. "Feaful hurry to go to Ganfie."

The other children caught her and heaved her back up on to her chair.

"Sit still," they said. "He's not your grandfather. You must say sir, or Mr Sylvester. He's only Anna's grandfather, not yours."

"But Soffytina wants a ganfie," Sofia insisted, jerking away. "Soffytina wants to be like Anna and have a ganfie like Anna."

"You *can't*," they said. "You can't, because he isn't *our* grandfather. He's our patron. He's only grandfather to Anna."

"But Soffytina wants a ganfie," said Sofia, starting to cry. "Wants ganfie. Soffytina wants." She struggled and suddenly jerked herself free. As quick as lightning, she ducked under the children's arms and set off after Anna.

"Anna . . . Anna . . . !" she cried. "Soffytina want ganfie too, ganfie, too!"

She caught up with Anna in the hall, clung to her and wiped her nose on Anna's lavender-blue dress.

"Anna, Anna, Anna! Soffytina wants Ganfie too, Ganfie for Soffytina too."

Anna pressed her to her and tried to stop her crying. She felt deeply unhappy.

"Yes, yes, my poppet, if only I could," she whispered.

The Patron came out and saw them there.

"What's the matter?" he said. "Why is the child crying?"

Anna put Sofia down. At the sight of the Patron's stern face and authoritative figure, she had been gripped with terror and hidden her head in the skirt of her dress.

"She says she wants a grandfather, too," Anna said truthfully, as the Patron always demanded clear and truthful replies to his questions.

The Patron frowned and looked confused.

"What? A grandfather?"

"Yes," said Anna, looking timid. "A grandfather, just as I have."

There was a silence, the child daring to peep out from behind Anna's skirt for a moment. She met the Patron's eyes and quickly hid herself again. Her plaits were sticking straight out round her head. The Patron looked at her and continued to appear somewhat bewildered.

Then he suddenly turned on his heel.

"Take the child to where she should be," he said to Anna, "and then let's have our coffee. I've been waiting for you."

Anna lifted Sofia, timid now, and slightly scared, and her brothers and sisters, listening trembling and terrified near the door, took her in hand again, all of them feeling relieved.

"You silly!" they said, hauling Sofia up on to her chair once more, rather heavy-handedly in relief after their fright, and Sofia Katrina at once snapped at them with her sharp little teeth.

"Soffytina *not* silly," she said furiously.

Seven

Mr Sylvester sat in silence as they drank their coffee, not even asking Anna where she had been all afternoon. In the end, Anna had to tell him herself, although she had promised Mademoiselle.

"I've been up to see Kari on the Common with a basket of food, because she's ill in bed," she said.

"Kari on the Common?" he said absently. He was not very interested in his inferiors and often could not remember their names. "Did Mademoiselle give you permission?"

"Yes," said Anna. "And Kari sends her most grateful thanks."

"Good," he said.

"She looked like a corpse," said Anna. "I think she needs a doctor."

The Patron's face clouded a little.

"The Common belongs to the parish and the manor has no obligations towards those who live there," he said. "Anyhow . . ." Then he remembered. ". . . Isn't Kari the mother of the boy who . . ." He fell silent, as if unwilling to speak about the insult he had received. But Anna understood all the same.

"Yes," she said, waiting fearfully as the Patron's face darkened even more. But he said nothing, the matter being altogether too unpleasant to mention. He drank a second cup in silence after Anna had poured it out for him from the silver coffee-pot. Then he suddenly asked her:

"What was her name again?"

"Who?" said Anna in confusion. "Do you mean Kari, Grandfather?"

"No, no," said the Patron impatiently. "I mean the little girl—the child—the one with the little plaits?"

"Oh," said Anna, smiling with delighted surprise, as he seldom asked about the children. "Her name's Sofia Katrina."

"Of course, yes," said the Patron, remembering that this was the child he had seen baptised in the church sacristy, and who had then bitten the minister's cheek. Suddenly, he smiled at the memory.

"A nice little girl," he said. "Is she good?"

"As good as gold," said Anna happily. Then after a moment's thought, she added: "But you have to treat her in the right way. Little children are like grown-ups. Some made one way, some another."

"You mean that you only find the gold after some perseverance?" said the Patron smiling.

"Yes," said Anna. "At least, one has to be interested and attentive and keep looking." She had read about gold-diggers in books from the Patron's shelves, and was not short of an answer. They both laughed, and the day that had begun so badly looked like improving towards evening.

In the midst of their laughter, Anna remembered Mats.

"If only he had the sense to come now," she thought. "Then it wouldn't be so difficult to clear it all up."

For the next few days, the Patron seemed more friendly towards the children. When he met them on the stairs or out of doors, he would stop and even say a few words, and once when he found Addie grooming his riding-horse in the stable and saw that he was doing it thoroughly and well, he thanked him with a pat on the head and said he was a clever little man. What did he want to be when he grew up?

"Coachman to the Patron, sir," Addie replied immediately in a loud voice, bowing from where he was standing on a step-ladder in order to be able to reach the horse's back. He had the scraper in one hand and the brush in the other and was using them alternately, just as he had learnt from the men. He put the dandruff and hairs he had removed in tidy heaps on the edge of the stall behind each horse, so that anyone could check how thoroughly the grooming had been done.

The Patron looked at him and smiled broadly.

"So you want to be Perman's successor, do you?" he said.

"Yes, please," said Addie, bowing again, his cheeks flapping and trembling as he eagerly set about the horse's hide again. He clambered up and down the step-ladder, sweating and brushing and rubbing, and there was not one speck of horse that was not shining, burnished and clean. Finally he fetched a great horn comb and carefully combed out the horse's mane, tail and hocks.

The Patron stood watching him for a while, and when Addie had finished and moved his ladder to the next stall, Mr Sylvester took a shining silver coin out of his pocket and gave it to him.

"Good work, little man," he said, in an unusually friendly voice. Addie thanked him, bowing and shuffling, so excited and agitated that he choked and could not get out a word.

Then after he had run round and shown the shining coin to everyone, the men, the maids, his brothers and sisters, he wrapped it in pink tissue paper and put it inside an old bark-box Mademoiselle had given him. He kept the box under his pillow and every Sunday, sometimes even more often, he took it out and held it in his hand just for the pleasure of looking at it. Sometimes he carried it about with him, tied into the corner of his handkerchief, but that was on Sundays only, of course, when things had to be extra grand in some way.

His brothers and sisters admired him greatly for his wealth. The men teased him, but Agda tossed her head, ill-tempered as usual.

"There you are," she said. "The Patron's generous enough when it comes to them brats. Showering money over them like that! But me what works and slaves away, he can't even give a farthing above me wages. No, he'd rather cut his fingers off, you can be sure of that."

The other children also noticed signs that the Patron's attitude to them was becoming slightly less hostile. John and the twins were once or twice taken to school in the carriage when the Patron had to be down in the village in the morning. Once he even went into the school and listened to a lesson. He asked Mr Bromander how the children were getting on. When Mr Bromander had nothing but good to say about them and also praised John for his industry and progress, the Patron looked pleased and satisfied. As he was in the village anyhow, he went to the store and bought a twist of striped peppermint-sticks for them. In the mornings when they all crowded round his doorway to say good morning, he was much less stern and severe than before. One day he even let Sofia step over the threshold and come in to shake his hand.

"Come on in, little girl," he said. "Let me have a look at you."

Sofia went in very carefully, on tiptoe. The floor was so shiny, you just couldn't know whether it wasn't going to suddenly crack and break under you like ice. Nothing was safe in a room where a troll lived in a cupboard on the wall. She curtseyed and scuttled round, bobbing in all directions, her quick brown eyes darting round the room.

"Mornin', mornin', everybody."

"Everybody?" said the Patron, laughing.

"Yes, everybody, mornin', mornin'," twittered Sofia, curtseying in all directions. There were so many people in the room, the elk on the wall, the bear on the floor, the big clock in the corner with its bulging stomach and narrow waist, looking just like a woman. And then the troll! You had to be terribly polite to trolls, otherwise you never knew what might happen.

"It's me you're supposed to be greeting," said the Patron, holding out his hand.

"Yes, mornin', mornin', Ganfie dear," said Sofia happily, standing on tiptoe and pressing a smacking great kiss on the Patron's chin.

Complete silence fell in the room, except for the great clock that just went on ticking in self-satisfaction without any sense of the horror of the moment. The children in the doorway gaped and drew back a little, ready to flee. Anna closed her eyes in lightning prayer—please, please let it be all right. The Patron himself looked just as bewildered as he had when Mats Kari spat in his face.

Then something happened. The troll in the telephone let out a couple of shrill signals that sounded as if it had exploded inside there. Brrrrrrrrrring! The children jumped nervously and moved back. Sofia let out a squeal and rushed up to the Patron, flung her arms round his neck and burrowed her head into his chest—was the troll after her? Brrrrrring! Brrrrrring! Yes, it was after her, help, help! She burrowed deeper and pushed and shoved, in terror trying to get right inside the Patron. She clung round his neck with her arms, and held on tightly with her legs. The Patron sat there as if caught in a clamp.

Anna rushed forward, lifted the telephone receiver off and said hullo. The troll calmed down for a moment. So did Sofia. At the sound of Anna's hullo, she stopped pushing and shoving, raised her face from the Patron's shirt-front and looked round inquisitively. Oh, so Anna had got the better of the troll, had she? Oh, well, then. Sofia slid down and ran over to her brothers and sisters, who quickly dragged her away with them to the pantry.

"You must be out of your mind," they kept saying, shaking her until she grew annoyed and snapped at them with her teeth.

"Soffytina *not* out of mind," she said.

But the children sat there trembling with anxiety over what would happen, and when Anna came out to them a few minutes later, they turned their pale faces towards her.

"Is he very angry, Anna?" they whispered. But she shook her head, looking quite happy.

"No," she said. "I don't think he's angry. His forehead's smooth, his eyes mild, and he didn't say anything. It's funny," she said, surprised herself.

"Yes," they said, wondering about it as they ate their porridge, John with a dreamy expression in his eyes.

"Just imagine if one day he even learnt to like us," he said. "Just think, if one day you really *felt* that he liked us all."

"Yes," they all said. "Just imagine."

"Yes," said Anna, with a sigh from the depths of her heart. Her greatest wish was that the Patron would love the other children as he loved her, and would stop making any difference between them and her.

"But you mustn't just think about taking," she added with her fourteen-year-old wisdom. "You have to think about giving something back, too."

"Yes," they said faintly, not really understanding. Addie said nothing at all and looked very suspicious, thinking about his silver coin. Give it back? Never.

"First you have to be the kind of person he *can* like," Anna said. "And before you can expect anything more, you have to feel grateful for what you've already been given. Do you understand what I mean?"

"Oh, yes," they all chorused, feeling genuinely grateful, Addie most of all because no one seemed to be after his wealth.

"We mustn't forget how difficult things were for us," said Anna. "What it was like at Kulla Croft sometimes, when Karlberg came home drunk, when Ida beat us with the broom, when Sofia was ill with hunger, and there wasn't a bit of flour or a single potato in the larder. And remember what it was like when you were lodged out in the parish!"

"Yes," they all said, looking wide-eyed back into the past, if only a few months. John remembered how the miller used to beat him with a leather strap—the terror and pain and degradation of it all. The twins held hands and hugged each other, just as they had done when the crofter had frightened them with his ranting. Addie's cheeks trembled tearfully as he thought what it would be like if he still lived at the Sound. Those rough farm boys who had thrown hard snowballs and stones at him would certainly have taken the silver coin off him—if he had even had one. Sofia remembered the dark cupboard she had been locked in, and her eyes darkened at the thought.

"Not there," she said. "Soffytina never go there again. Always with Anna and Ganfie. Soffytina always be with Anna and dear Ganfie."

"Sssh," they said to her, still afraid of her impudence at addressing their patron as Grandfather.

But inside, in secret, each of them tried out what it felt like to be able to say the word.

Eight

The change in Mr Sylvester was indeed remarkable. He had always been sharp and impatient at the slightest thing, but now he was occasionally quite cheerful and amusing. The melancholy that had afflicted him for many years began to lift and melt like snow. They noticed it from one day to the next, just as the real snow melted out in the countryside.

"Come in, come in," he said in the mornings as they crowded round the doorway. "Come on in. Don't just stand there."

When they politely and respectfully gathered round him, he looked at them kindly and asked questions and listened with interest to their answers. He held Sofia between his knees and put his big gold watch to her ear for her to listen. He was neither irritable nor cross when each morning she firmly and obstinately tripped across the room and gave him a smacking kiss on his chin, saying: "Mornin', mornin', dear Ganfie."

"Let her be," he said, chuckling at her.

Sofia swung her skirts, looking triumphantly at her brothers and sisters.

"He says let her be," she repeated, almost bursting with importance.

"Soffytina's got a ganfie now, just like Anna," she kept saying, tossing her plaits, pirouetting round, holding her skirts and flashing her eyes, proud and happy.

"Little show-off!" muttered Agda crossly, ill-tempered at the very sight of the child. "Showing off like a dancer from the big city. Horrible little beast."

If she could do so without Mademoiselle seeing her, she would slap the child and pull her hair and be nasty to her, because she could not endure these slummy crofter's brats being at the manor as if they were children of the rich, allowing Agda to serve them. If anything in the world was unjust, then that was.

But when Agda pinched her or pulled her hair, Sofia at once forgot her fine manners and rushed wildly at the maid-servant, screaming and scratching and biting, giving as good as she got. Then Agda told tales and complained.

"Horrid little beast, that brat is," she said.

But it was easy to put up with a smack now and again from Agda when she had a "ganfie", as Anna had. You didn't have to be in the kitchen all day. Sofia discovered that as long as she was careful and walked quietly and didn't make a noise, Mr Sylvester had no objections to her being in the room.

"Oh, so you're in here?" he said, the first time he found her perched on a chair in the drawing-room, looking at the picture of Annemaria Beatrice. He was frowning and about to say something harsh, because the child's presence in the drawing-room went beyond his orders.

But Sofia slipped off the chair, curtseyed to him and pirou-etted round in front of him.

"Yes, Ganfie dear, Soffytina here," she said, sitting down again, neatly and tidily on the edge of the chair. The Patron tried to hide a smile, looking sternly at her and trying to be even more severe.

"Shouldn't you ask permission from me first?" he said.

"Yes, please, dear Ganfie," she said cheerfully.

Then the Patron smiled and when Mademoiselle came limping in to fetch the child from the forbidden area, he said:

"Let her be. Let her stay. It's all right."

What a child! She was like a ray of sunlight falling on the Patron's heart, melting the crust of ice round it. It happened all so naturally that he hardly noticed it himself. He felt warm life returning inside him, just as the frozen earth must feel when the spring sun melted the ice crust and could breathe again after its long sleep.

Mademoiselle and the servants, the children and Anna, all noticed the change that slowly came over the Patron. The atmosphere in the great house became freer and happier than it had been for many years. Mademoiselle, so used to limping round and sighing for the good old days, now moved more lightly, humming good-humouredly, thinking that things were actually improving again.

"Spring's coming to the manor," she said. "Spring's coming at last."

"At last!" said the Patron, laughing. "You're optimistic. It's only the beginning of April still, so we can't expect much."

Then he went out on to the veranda steps and stood looking at the crocuses and snowdrops cautiously sticking up in the lawn, although there were still thin patches of snow lying round them. He drew the scent of melting snow into his nostrils and breathed deeply. John and the twins were just coming home from school, and he called out to them.

"Look," he said, pointing up at the sky, where a formation of birds was flying north. The cranes were back, and their strange calls filled the air long after they had disappeared over the forest ridge.

Anna came out holding Sofia by the hand, tempted by the strange calls of the birds, and Addie came leaping across the stable-yard, wanting to see, too. The Patron gathered them round him and stood there for a long time, telling them about the cranes, those rare timid birds that sometimes held secret meetings deep inside the forest or far away on the desolate heaths, where people seldom went. At these meetings, they held a ball, dancing peculiar dances, and they were so frightened of being disturbed that they always set out guards to ensure that no one saw them.

The children listened with rapt attention, John with his head forward and his hand cupped behind his ear, his eyes on the Patron's lips.

"Just imagine," they said later. "He talked to us all that time. *All that time*." The fact that the Patron had spoken to them for such a long spell was far more extraordinary than what he actually said to them.

Anna went round almost holding her breath with delight. She now realised how difficult the first months had been, the Patron's hostility to the children filling her days with anxiety, as she saw them creeping about like timid little animals in their anxiety to please. She thought again about the Patron's heart, as Mademoiselle had described it; how it had been in a desert so long that it had withered and died.

"Now it's come alive again," she thought. "Now it's

beginning to wake up and live." And she smiled to herself at the thought of how they would make it open out and blossom. They would help, all of them.

"We mustn't just take," she said to the children. "We must try to give something back too, from the heart, of what we have in our hearts."

"Yes, let's give our hearts," said the children, eagerly and willingly, Addie too, for as long as he was allowed to keep his silver coin, he would much prefer to give his heart. John just looked dreamy.

"Now we're on the right road," he said, pushing aside his red fringe. "Now we're on the road to the gardens of Paradise. You know, Anna, sometimes it's like glimpsing something or hearing a song or catching a scent."

Anna smiled at him and nodded as she tied the ribbons in Sofia's plaits. Sofia had as usual managed to untie them and ruffle her hair in a vain attempt to turn her straight locks into curls.

"Yes, John, you know, don't you?" she said. Nowadays, she never doubted when John dreamt his old dream of Paradise and the Garden of Eden, the wonderful gardens at the end of the world. Whoever had struggled hard against need and privation and learnt to sacrifice and deny himself, and yet had eyes that lit up and lips that smiled—that person knew the Garden of Eden existed. Anna was no longer a child. She was fourteen and had learnt a great deal. Somewhere, far away or close to, there was something that gave you strength when you were weakening. John called it the Garden of Eden and to him the strength came like a scent or a note from a distance. Others called it by another name and felt in a different way. But for all those who nourished a longing in their hearts, the

Garden of Eden stood there in bloom at the end of the world.

The Patron was so friendly and kind that it was truly remarkable. The crofters and day-workers who came to his office to beg for credit for half a sack of potatoes or a little rye, because their stores and lofts and cellars at home were empty, never stopped wondering about it. Before, when they had appealed to his mercy and told him how many children's mouths they had to feed at home, he used to reply sharply.

"It's not my fault you have so many children," he had said.

But now he was quite different. Now he asked how many children they had and how old they were. And no one with small children at home went without help from the manor.

"It's like a miracle," they said.

Foreman Germaine came in and asked what should be done about Mats Kari, as it looked as if they were not going to be able to find him. Once or twice the men had seen him up on the edge of the forest, looking down towards the manor, but as soon as they called, he had vanished into the forest, so quickly that it had been impossible to catch him. He was never at home in the cottage. Foreman Germaine had been there in person once or twice, but the boy had kept away and the sick woman had refused to say where he was, although Germaine had shouted and raved at her, using his sternest manner. She had just stared at him, mumbling and plucking at the covers with her fingers like an idiot.

"Couldn't get a sensible word out of her," he said. Then he asked what the Patron suggested next. Should he perhaps put a guard on the cottage? The wretched boy was bound to go indoors at some time or other.

But the Patron gestured dismissively.

"Let the boy be," he said. "I've no wish to see him again."

"But he must be punished," said Germaine, offended and righteously indignant.

"Leave him alone," said the Patron, wishing to end the conversation.

"But he must have a good thrashing,' said Germaine, acting the good servant removing all the weeds from his master's fields. "A thrashing he remembers for the rest of his life, thief and spitter that he is . . ."

They were incautious words. The Patron did not wish to be reminded of his humiliation. He suddenly grew angry and slapped the table so hard that the inkpot jumped.

"Listen to what I say, my man!" he said. "Leave the boy be. When all is said, he's only a child. Let him be. I do not wish to think about the matter again."

At that he waved the foreman impatiently away and Germaine left.

"So that's how it is, is it?" he said to Agda. "That's all the thanks you get for doing your duty. Just shouted at and angry words, that's all you get."

But Anna had heard the conversation. She ran out to Mademoiselle and asked if she could again go up to Kari with a basket of food.

"But you've just been there," said Mademoiselle. However sick Kari was, she had to think before wasting things. It was unfair to give too much to one person when poverty and need were everywhere, she thought, and the Common didn't even belong to the manor.

But as she protested and made objections, annoyed with Anna, she was nevertheless packing up a bag of eggs, some bread and a pat of butter.

"There you are," she said. "Get along now and come back

quickly. I can't have you running about the forest after dark."

Then she called after Anna, who was already outside the door, and asked her if she had her gaiters on, and her cardigan and a proper cap.

"Don't you come back with a cold, that's all I say," she said.

"Oh, no, I won't," said Anna patiently, far too hot in her woollen cardigan as she ran.

Nine

The sky was bright and high above the pines, the melting snow rushing along between hillocks of moss, heather and bilberry bushes. As Anna ran past Dally-Peter's cottage, the little old man was standing outside sunning himself, his goat there, too, and three small pearl-grey hens walking round pecking at what they could find. Anna stopped and greeted him, as she always did when she went past his cottage.

"Good day, good day. How are you?" she called up to him, her voice light and cheerful.

"Thank you, as well with me as with you," the old man called back. He sounded cheerful, too.

"Love from baby Sofia," said Anna, calling up to him from where she was on the forest path. "She's growing into a big girl now."

"That's as it should be," said the old man, stroking his beard. "Give her my love."

"Yes, I will. Goodbye now. I haven't time to stop today," she went on. "I've got to find out how things are with Kari on the Common. I've food for her, a few eggs and that sort of thing, that Mademoiselle thinks she can eat."

"Then you'd better hurry," said the old man.

The cottage on the Common sat there with its brown walls and white chimney like a gingerbread house. No one was about, nor was there any sign of smoke. The Common was quite silent, apart from the distant sound of a bubbling brook. Anna walked carefully round the cowshed and peered before daring to cross the yard in front of the house, remembering the hard snowball of the previous time.

However, she got there unharmed, and as no one answered her knock, she opened the door. It creaked and protested as if it had a bad dose of rheumatism in its rusty hinges. She stopped in the doorway and blinked against the dim light inside.

"Good day," she cried cheerfully. "Here I am again. Mademoiselle sent me up with a few things for you, and wonders how you are."

The cottage was quite silent and no one answered her. But when her eyes had become accustomed to the light, she saw that Mats was sitting on a wooden chair over by Kari's bed. He turned his head and stared at her, but said nothing. Anna went closer, afraid of frightening the boy away. But he was sitting quite still, hunched up on the chair, only the eyes in his thin dirty face following her movements.

"Good day," said Anna again, as quietly and gently as she could. She put the food-bag down on the table. "Lovely day today. A real spring day, it is."

There was no reply to that, either. Suddenly she was aware of the unnatural silence. She looked over towards the bed. At least Kari might say something. But she was lying quite still, staring straight ahead.

Anna suddenly heard herself scream, and the sound was so

frightening in the silence that the boy jerked out of his paralysis. He leapt up and screamed too, and with his arm over his face, he fled out of the cottage.

Anna followed him in panic, stumbling over the high step. Out! She must get outside! "Mats!" she called. "Mats!" She stretched her hands out towards him, wanting to hold him, because he was alive and like her. The other person in there was dead.

But Mats fled away from her and ran beyond the outhouses. Anna stopped in the middle of the yard, the radiant spring day bringing her to her senses. She drew a deep breath and felt her heart thumping.

"What a way to behave," she said to herself. She wiped her forehead, trying to breathe more evenly, then turned back to the cottage.

Calmly and sensibly, she stepped into the room. She had not been afraid of Mother Kari when she was alive, and there was no earthly reason why she should be so now that she was dead. Everyone had to die, Anna too, when the time came. A dead body was just a body that had stopped living.

Anna had seen a dead person before, old Greatgran, who had stopped living when Karlberg had wanted to send her to the poor-house. Anna knew what she had to do. A worn old psalm-book lay on the table by the window. She pushed it under Kari's chin, then carefully closed the dead woman's eyes and crossed her hands over her chest.

Then she cleaned up the room so that it would be tidy when people came. Pieces of boiled turnip lay in a bowl on the shelf above the stove, so she took them out to the porch cupboard together with the food Mademoiselle had sent. She shook the tablecloth and moved a pot-plant from the window and placed it beside Kari. It was a fuchsia covered with flowers. It was the only lovely thing in the shabby cottage, and she thought Kari ought to have it beside her.

When she had finished, she went over and curtseyed to the dead woman, for there were people who believed that a person's soul did not go to heaven immediately, but stayed in the earthly body until it had been placed in consecrated ground.

"Goodbye, Mother Kari," she whispered. "I'll speak to the Patron about Mats. I'm sure something can be done for him."

Mats was in the woodshed when she came out. He had pulled the door to so as not to be seen, but his sobs betrayed him. After thinking for a moment, Anna went in to see him.

"Mats," she said. "You'd better come with me."

Mats took his hands away from his face, which was streaked with tears. But his eyes were wild and defiant.

"What for?" he said, trying to sound scornful, but his voice trembling and unsteady.

"You can't stay here alone," said Anna.

"Yes, I can," he replied sharply, swallowing his tears. But then they rose again and overcame him. He lowered his head and wept.

"They told Mum . . . about them eggs and all that with the Patron. She knowed all about it . . . they told her that . . . that . . . that I were a thief and she couldn't bear that. She cried all day. Then she died. She's dead . . . Mum's *dead*."

"Yes, yes," said Anna, sitting down beside him on a log.

"She's dead. And it were that German what . . . he came and shouted it all out . . . so she knowed and were miserable . . ."

Mats suddenly stopped crying.

"I'll kill him," he shouted. "I'll kill him!"

"Yes, yes," said Anna, reluctant to remonstrate. "But in the meantime, it'd be best if we talked to the Patron, so that you get your job back and have somewhere to live."

Mats lowered his head again.

"I spat at him," he whispered.

"You can ask pardon for that," said Anna, thinking hopefully about how friendly the Patron had been recently.

"Never!" said Mats, trying to keep back the tears again. He wiped his nose on the back of his hand and swallowed and swallowed. Suddenly he turned angrily on Anna sitting there watching his misery.

"What are you sitting here for?" he said. "Get off to where you belong."

"I'm waiting for you," said Anna. "I thought we could go together."

"Then you'll have to wait till doomsday," said Mats.

"I don't think I can wait that long," said Anna, smiling slightly. "But I've time to wait for a little while longer."

They sat there on the woodpile in the shed until dusk began to fall. As the sun went down, it grew colder, and Anna was glad of her gaiters and woollen cardigan. Mats sat hunched up, sometimes weeping violently sometimes quite quiet. The light went from the heath and the windows of the cottage grew dark and dead. The boy suddenly shuddered.

"If only I'd somewhere to go," he whispered.

Anna got up.

"Let's go then," she said, and this time he at once came with her.

Ten

They walked in silence through the forest, twigs crackling under their feet, as it was freezing again now the sun had gone. Mats's teeth were chattering and he was shaking with cold, grief and loss. Anna was cold, too, worried about what she had undertaken. But then she straightened up.

"Dear Lord, please help us," she prayed. "Mats couldn't possibly stay up there alone."

Halfway to the manor, John came to meet them. Mademoiselle had been worrying and had sent him off, he said, and the Patron had asked after Anna twice.

"Dear Lord," thought Anna, frightened again.

When the manor's brightly lit windows came in sight as they left the forest, Mats stopped, panic-stricken.

"I daren't!" he exclaimed. "I daren't. No, I'm going back." Then he looked into the forest, where it was dense and black between the trees, the smell of damp and ice rising from the wet moss. He took two steps in that direction, stopped, and stood still, trembling. Then he turned again.

"I daren't go back, neither," he whispered.

Anna put out her hand, and although Mats was fourteen and already a working labourer, he took it in the dark.

The Patron was in his office with the foreman, discussing the spring work on the farms. They stared as Mats and Anna came in, the Patron's monocle falling out of his eye, then dangling and swinging on its cord.

"What's all this?" he said sharply.

"Mats's mother's dead," said Anna, looking the Patron straight in the eye. She stepped forward, leaving Mats by the door. He started weeping bitterly again at Anna's words, the tears falling unhindered on to his hands.

Silence fell in the room. The foreman stared and the Patron stared. Mats put his cap over his face to hide himself.

"And so you've brought him here?" said the Patron gesturing toward Mats as if Anna had dragged in a rotting carcase.

"Yes. He couldn't stay up there alone," said Anna. "And then there are one or two things he has to clear up."

She looked at Mats, who gave a numb, jerky bow, his shoulders shaking, his trousers patched all over and ragged between the patches. It was a pitiful sight. The Patron felt a sudden distaste and anger, but he controlled himself. He had told the foreman that the matter was settled.

"Well, say what you've come to say. Say it and then go," he said impatiently.

But the boy just bowed behind his cap, bowing and shuffling and looking wretched, unable to get out a word. Anna had to help him again.

"He can't speak because of his tears," she said, leaning towards the Patron. "But it's about those eggs and all that."

"Oh, well," said the Patron hastily, as he did not want

"all that" dragged up again. "All right, then. You can go."

Mats bowed again behind his cap, weeping still.

"But he's got nowhere to go," said Anna. "May he stay here?"

"Yes, yes," said the Patron, uneasy at Mats's pitiful weeping. "He can stay here overnight. Then we'll talk about it again tomorrow."

"Thank you," said Anna.

They went out to Mademoiselle and Mats was given some pea soup and pork left over from dinner. Although he was thinking about his mother all the time, the tears falling into his soup, he ate everything put before him, for he was starving hungry. Afterwards, he had no wish to sleep with the others in the labourers' quarters, so he went out to the stables and lay down in some hay in an empty stall. John and Anna went out and sat with him for a while, so that he should not feel too lonely.

But in the kitchen, Germaine was having his evening meal with the labourers, and he was angry. He had wanted to tell the Patron how unwise it would be to have a thief at the manor, but the Patron had cut him short without listening.

"He's bewitched by that girl," said Germaine. "She seems to decide everything now. Soon we'll have to go bowing and scraping for her advice about ploughing and carting and all. It's not right."

"But she's got a good heart," said one of the maids. "Things have been better in lots of ways since she came. Sort of lighter than before, if you knows what I mean."

"That's what *you* think," said Agda scornfully. "That's all right for you, but what about me? Me's the one what has to see to those brats she's brought in. Things ain't no lighter for me, I'll have you know. And that little beast, scratching and biting, what'd you give me for her, eh? I agree, it's not right."

"Oh, you keep causing trouble with her all the time," said the girls, laughing, which made Agda angrier than ever.

"You've all had your heads turned," she said. "Me causing trouble? I've never heard the likes of it. Me, causing trouble. What a label to get!"

"You could get a worse one. You could be blamed for other things," said Germaine, a meaningful glint in his yellow cat-eyes. "What about that business of the missing pork and sausages the other week? You free from suspicion of having taken *them*?"

"I've never heard the likes of it!" cried Agda, her throat flushing with indignation. "So now I'm to be called a thief, too, am I? I said someone were following me about that time. And well I know who it was, too."

"But not everyone knows that. The boy's back again now," said the foreman, spreading himself a thick piece of bread and butter. The labourers and maidservants took in his words and thought it all wrong that Mats was back again. Weren't there plenty of boys to be had without the Patron taking in thieves? And what about all the rest of them, now? They might get blamed for what Mats had done, just as the foreman had said about Agda and the stuff missing from the store. No, things weren't right, that they weren't.

"Me, who's never as much as taken a pin in all my life!" said Agda, flushing right down to the neck of her dress with indignation.

Eleven

In the office, Mr Sylvester was equally perplexed over his own behaviour. Allowing Mats to leave his work and escape punishment was one thing. There were unpleasant aspects of the whole business that he preferred not to touch on. He had wished to have nothing more to do with the boy, or hear anything more about him.

But now the boy was suddenly back under the manor roof again, living off the Patron, from who he had stolen, and whom he had insulted in a shameful manner. The Patron had neither reproved him nor spoken a harsh word to him, just taken him back and let him go off as if nothing had happened.

"It's insane," he thought as he sat there alone, his monocle in his eye, staring at the mirror on the wall in front of him, as if trying to discover just where in himself the insanity lay. All his life, he had been proud of being a stern master, to whom everyone humbly bowed. He had always been hard on his employees and had punished them severely for the sins that had come to his knowledge. There had been occasions when he had personally thrashed his labourers with his own riding-crop, and the mere sight of the ruler on his desk had made grown men turn pale and tremble. For lesser sins than those Mats had committed, he had driven crofters and indented labourers away from the manor, out of their homes, wife, children, furniture and all. He had been without mercy, inflexible in his demands and sterner than most masters, and this had always been a matter of pride to him.

"But what has happened to me?" he thought now, staring at his own reflection. He rose from the desk and went closer, running his hand over his grey hair and staring at his own face. It suddenly occurred to him that a change really had come over him. His forehead was smooth, his brow unlined, and his mouth, before so thin and hard, had softened, the corners turned upwards beneath his moustache.

"What's this? Am I standing here laughing at things?" he thought, frightened at himself. He hurriedly frowned with impatience as of old and pressed his lips into a straight line. Then he flung his cloak over his shoulder and went out.

He met Mademoiselle in the hall. She was so startled by his grim appearance that she anxiously asked herself what was going on now, because she had not seen him look like that for a long time. The Patron did not speak to her, but went into the kitchen to see if Mats were still there. The men were still sitting round the table, chatting cheerfully with the maids. When they saw the Patron's face, they fell silent so abruptly that it was as if a thread had been cut. The foreman was quicker on the uptake and rose to his feet, telling the men sharply to go and get on with feeding the animals and arranging the barn for the night.

"You lot going to sit here all night?" he said, showing his

Patron what an industrious man he was. The maids rushed round the kitchen, clattering plates, pouring water into the bowls and scraping pans, as if they worked like that every day of their lives and hardly had time even to draw breath.

The Patron asked after Mats and when he was told where he was, he went out to the stables, frowning on the way and clamping his mouth shut in an attempt to appear stern. When the day-workers in the stable-yard saw his face, they quickly vanished round corners and into sheds to escape his wrath.

"What's going on?" they said to themselves, staring after him. "What's wrong with him? Has he gone back to his old self?" Two crofters who had been trying to decide all day whether they dared go to the office and ask for some seed on credit, now decided that it was pointless and hurried home empty-handed.

Mats Kari lay in an empty stall in the stable, curled up in some hay, and round him sat the children trying to comfort him. Anna had put an old horse-blanket over him and tried to make him comfortable. John was sitting by his head talking quietly to him. The twins and Addie and Sofia had also made their way there, anxious to be where the others were. They were kneeling in the hay, staring silently at the hunched weeping figure. The horses were standing in their boxes, their heads hanging sleepily, their tails flicking and their hoofs thudding on the floor. Clio, the foal, scraped her feet against the box wall, trying to get her head over the edge. She could smell the presence of people and had no desire to sleep.

No one noticed the Patron as he stepped inside. Dusk had fallen over the stables and the spring evening was dark blue outside. Warm steam was rising from the horses. Four fair heads, Anna's, the twins' and Addie's, looked like great white flowers planted in the straw. The two red heads, John's and Sofia's, melted into the dimness and looked blurred. The figure underneath the horse-blanket was like any old heap except that sobs came from it spasmodically. John's gentle boyish voice filled the spaces with comforting words. As he was deaf, he always spoke louder than necessary, and the Patron stopped to listen.

"The air is as clear as crystal and warm at the same time, filled with scents from the flowering gardens. It's so easy to breathe there, and when you move, your body feels as light as if you were floating . . . "

"She found it so hard to breathe . . ." came from the horse-blanket. "She were breathless like some poor old dog . . ."

". . . It's full of the most beautiful flowers," John went on. "And you can pick the most wonderful fruit from the trees, juicy and refreshing. Better than the reddest Christmas apple, oh, yes. And the trees bend down and offer their fruit to anyone who wants it . . ."

". . . She couldn't eat nothing but yolks of eggs at the end," came from the horse-blanket. "And when the German had been up and told her I stoled them, she wouldn't eat no more. Not even them mamzelle sent up. No, she wouldn't touch not another egg. As if she'd gone off them, like . . ."

". . . In the mornings the dew lies on the grass like pearls and there's bright butterflies and happy children playing everywhere. And when the wind comes in from the sea, it brings with it the most amazing music—the ringing and tinkling of tens of thousands of silver bells in the distance . . ."

"This morning," hiccoughed the dark heap under the blanket. "She says to me, open the door, Mats, boy, she says. I wants to hear them church bells. And I runs to open it but it weren't Sunday and you couldn't hear nothing and I tells her. But she says all the same open the door wider, Mats, boy, because they're ringing now and I does want to hear them . . ."

"She was probably hearing the silver bells of Paradise," said Anna, adjusting the horse-blanket. Sofia was sitting at Mats's feet and at once fussily pulled at another corner of it.

"Yes, Matsie," she said firmly. "Silver blells of Paladise, that's what they was."

"If only I could believe that," said Mats. "If only I could believe that were true. All that stuff about the Garden of Eden. That Mum were there now. But . . ." he buried his face again in the hay. "I know she's lying up there in that cold dark cottage. And she's all alone and dead . . ."

"That's just her body," said Anna. "Her soul's somewhere else. She heard the bells, didn't she? You said that. And that was when the gates of Paradise opened for her. She's in those gardens now, sure as sure. Don't worry about your mother, Mats. She's all right now."

"Ooh, yes, Matsie. She all right now," said Sofia. "She all right now."

"Be quiet!" said the twins, nudging her. "Be quiet, you silly thing."

At that moment they looked behind them and saw the Patron standing there, listening. They whispered to the others, but John, who couldn't hear them, went on speaking in his clear gentle voice that seemed to make his childish words shimmer in the dark. As if the boy were sitting there threading pearls on a string, the Patron thought, and then he sighed. His frown had already gone.

"It's there for the living as well as for the dead," John was saying. "They can find strength and peace and joy there, they can. It's all there for everyone with a soul and a longing in his heart. But it's far away, right at the end of the world, and the road can be hard and difficult. Each person has to find his own way and there's lots of ways. The poor man has his and the rich man his, the warrior his and the child his. But for all of them it's the same—only those who yearn hard enough get there . . ."

One of the children nudged John and he fell silent. The dim light in the stable dispersed and obliterated the pearls the Patron had seen. He sighed again, despite himself. Anna got up, brushed the hay off her dress and went over to him.

"We've been talking to Mats for a while," she explained looking up at him, not really sure of his expression in the dark. She felt a stab of anxiety in case he was angry.

"I'm sorry I've been out here too long, Grandfather dear," she said, feeling for his hand. Sofia, missing nothing, ran forward and clutched his other hand.

"Sowwy, Ganfie dear," she said. The other children tried to pull her away, as you never knew how long the Patron would tolerate such behaviour.

"Sofia! *Don't*, Sofia!" they said, pulling at her skirt.

But Sofia pressed the Patron's hand to her heart, holding on tight to his thumb and middle finger, kicking out at them.

"Leave me be with Ganfie," she said. "Want to be with Ganfie."

"Yes, leave her be, by all means," said Mr Sylvester, striving in vain to regain his stern mood.

Mats had got up and was standing there in his rags, covered with hay, his arms loose at his sides. He was staring down at the floor, unwilling to look at the Patron, but feeling a little better now. Although he had worked with men and learnt to swear and spit like them, he had found the childish words of comfort consoling. The story of the Garden of Eden had heartened him, somehow making his grief less bitter.

"Hm," said the Patron. "Are you all right here?"

"Yes, thank you," mumbled Mats.

"Well, that's all right then," said the Patron, embarrassed by his own friendliness. "Well, let's go, children. It's late."

"Yes, 'et's go," said Sofia, bobbing about by his hand. Anna turned to Mats, and the other children did so, too.

"Good night," she said. "Sleep well."

"Good night, good night," they said all together. "Sleep well, Mats."

"Good night, my boy," said the Patron, joining in the chorus.

"Good night," whispered Mats, bowing so that hay scattered in all directions. As the Patron, surrounded by the children, walked over to the door, he stepped down from the hay and followed silently behind them. The Patron noticed and turned round.

"What is it?" he said, looking at Mats, who had stopped and was timidly gazing at the floor.

"It was . . . just . . . *sorry*," he stammered.

"Yes, yes," said the Patron, suddenly touched against his will. "I'm sorry, too," he went on. "I shouldn't have hit you until I knew what the situation was."

But when he went out into the stable-yard, the chilly evening air caught him unawares. He noticed he had tears in his eyes and was angry with himself again.

"I must have gone mad," he thought. "What's happening to me?"

But within himself, somewhere underneath all his annoyance and astonishment, was a quiet stream of warmth and peace. He turned to the children stumping along at a respectful distance behind him, only Sofia daring to be so familiar as to hold his hand.

"John," he said, bending down and speaking into John's ear. "Didn't you once say you wanted to be a minister?"

"Yes," said John, flushing slightly. "But it was only a fancy thought," he added, because he was a year older now and knew that wishing and being were not the same thing.

But the Patron nodded encouragingly to him.

"You go on thinking that thought," he said. "Perhaps you'll have your wish granted one day."

When the children were standing by the veranda steps to say good night before going in through the kitchen entrance, he nodded at John again.

"Perhaps, John," he said. And it sounded like a promise.

Later that evening, after the maids had stopped clattering about in the kitchen and the house was silent, Anna crept across to the children's room and sat for a long time on the edge of John's bed, holding his hand. They couldn't talk, because the little children were asleep and if John were to hear, they would have had to talk so loudly that they would have disturbed them. But as they sat there holding each other's hands, they knew full well what they would like to have said. They were both so pleased about the Patron and the change that had occurred in him.

"It's as you said, Anna," whispered John. "If you want someone to like you, you have to give of your own heart first. Then the other heart will come to meet you. It's just as if he'd begun to like us, Anna."

"Yes," said Anna, nodding, and it rang through her like a song.

Twelve

Spring came quickly both indoors and outdoors at the manor. The Patron's forehead remained smooth as he greeted the children in the mornings, and the sight of Sofia's little plaits bobbing about made him smile. He stopped making such demands on Anna's time, no longer jealous of her, nor insisting on her presence for days on end. He had such a wealth inside him that he felt he could afford to share her.

"Yes, off you go then, if you want to," he said when she asked him if she could go and see some of her old friends in the cottages, or visit someone who was ill at the poor-house. "And tell Mademoiselle. Perhaps she'll give you something to take with you," he would add, without her having to ask him.

In the same way, without having to be asked, one day he dealt out seed-potatoes to all his crofters, a gift that was manna from heaven to them at this time of year, just when they were wondering how they were ever going to make out. Because their families had eaten all theirs.

"Nothing but a miracle," they said, staring up at the blue

spring sky and calling down blessings on their Patron, suddenly so good to his people.

"It's the spring," said Mademoiselle. "At last spring has come." She scuttled about like a youngster, not worrying at all about her swollen foot. There was so much to do at this time of year. Laundry saved up all through the winter had to be done in a grand wash, and steam from the boilers billowed out in great clouds from the wash-house. Down by the river, crofters' wives rinsed the newly-washed linen, slapping it with their wooden beaters, the sound echoing right up to Kulla ridge and resounding so that it sounded like a great troll up in the forest beating his seven-league carpets.

Then there was the spring-cleaning. Every corner from cellar to attic in the great white mansion was scrubbed and cleaned and polished. Anna put on an apron, too, tied a kerchief round her head and helped with all her heart. The maidservants had to admit that even they, grown women that they were, could hardly match the thoroughness of her work.

"She's an amazing one, that Miss Anna," they said to each other, with admiration in their voices. Only Agda tossed her head and did not agree.

"Why should it be so amazing that she can work?" she said. "She comes from an ordinary croft, just like us."

"Yes, but just because of that," the others said. They knew full well that if the same destiny had befallen them, they would certainly have taken the opportunity of doing nothing every minute of the day.

The children also helped wherever they could. John carried water and wood for the maids when he came back from school, and every evening he filled the drying cupboard with sticks for the next day. But when the men got him to help with the spring slaughter and gave him a pail of blood from the slaughtered pigs to whip, he turned pale and ill and had to leave them. The men laughed and teased him.

"Of course, you'd prefer to live off them juicy fruits what grows in them gardens of yours," they said, grinning. They often got John to talk about his dreams and then poked fun at him. They didn't really mean to be unpleasant, but they thought it comical that a child should go round talking like that.

"Pity that there place is so far away you can't get there in your meal-break," they used to say. "It'd be quite a way to go, wouldn't it now, all the way to the end of the world every time. You'll have to make do with a bit of black pudding and pork just like the rest of us."

Then they would laugh again so that it echoed round the barn walls, and take a bit of snuff and start hustling the next pig out of the sty and over to the slaughtering bench.

Mats Kari was the only one who didn't laugh as he silently and timidly went about his work with the others. He was often seen gazing up towards the forest ridge, thinking about his childhood home and his mother, whom they had buried in the churchyard. He thought about America, where his brothers and sisters had gone. It all merged into an aching longing in his heart and he felt confused and lonely and homeless. So for him, it was a comfort to think about the gardens of Paradise.

"For both the living and the dead. Yes, for everyone who has a soul and a longing in his heart," he thought. It had become a kind of link between heaven and earth to him, giving him a feeling that his mother was not so dead or distant as he sometimes thought.

"What are you standing there mooning about? Thinking up some more thievery, I suppose?" shouted the foreman, who had suddenly appeared and seen the boy's absent-minded look. The men glanced hastily at Mats, remembering that they had a thief among them, and the maidservants hurriedly felt their brooches to see if they were still there.

But Mats Kari himself noticed everything and looked at the foreman with hatred. He at once forgot everything that was beautiful, and instead thought ugly thoughts about Foreman Germaine and hell.

"I'll help him on his way there one day," he told Addie, who had become his confidant because of his constant presence in the stables. Addie nodded. At six years of age, he was going to be no less a man than fourteen-year-old Mats.

"Tell me when you going to do it," said Addie. "And I'll give you a hand." He puffed out his chest and wished he was as big as a grown man. He had also got on the wrong side of the foreman and had been beaten and sworn at, so thoughts of revenge weren't far from his mind.

The stables had a number of empty boxes at this time, because the horses were now working at full stretch out in the fields and there was nothing else for Addie to do except look after Clio, who had not yet been broken in and could not work. Clio was an exceptionally beautiful animal and was going to be a riding horse. Her mother was the black mare Regina had ridden to death over the ravine, the autumn before the children had been taken into the manor.

Addie devoted all his love to Clio now, grooming her four or five times a day, brushing and rubbing until the little foal shone like polished porphyry. He watered and fed her and daily took her out into the paddock and watched over her.

Old Perman, the coachman, had begun to be weary and tired, so he was glad to have such excellent help.

But the constant companionship of an animal as noble as Clio put ideas of grandeur into Addie's head. He began to regard his dream of becoming a coachman and sitting on the coachman's box in uniform as simple-minded. Coachman! He might just as well become a knight or a hussar, galloping along at breakneck speed on the back of fiery Clio, in shining boots and with a sword at his side. No longer was it Addie's greatest pleasure to sit up beside Perman, holding the reins under his leadership. Addie had grander ideas.

Secretly, he took Clio out to the field behind the barn, where he was hidden from sight on one side by the long wall of the barn, and by the forest on the other. There he clambered up on to the foal's back, using a rein slung across her back as a stirrup. But although they were good friends, the little horse was at once frightened and threw him. Addie hit his head on the ground and knocked out a tooth.

That didn't worry him very much, as it would have come out in time anyhow. So when he had recovered, he climbed up on one side and promptly fell off on the other. Clio seemed disturbed by his new way of keeping her company. But in the end she realised that it was a game and was meant to be fun. She stood still while he clambered up on her back, then she neighed delightedly, kicked out and threw him.

But Addie learnt something each time and one day he managed to stay mounted as long as it took to count to ten. He reckoned he had won the day then, because he did not dare keep the horse away from the stables any longer, in case anyone should notice. But just as he was about to slide off, he caught his leg in the home-made stirrup and couldn't get free. At that moment, Clio heard a horse whinny somewhere far away and set off with a leap in that direction. Addie hung on for a while, but on the stable road, he met the foreman and two men and fell off right at their feet. He landed in a puddle and covered himself with mud. The men laughed loudly. But the foreman picked him up by the collar and ducked him in the water trough. He ducked him twice and then beat him soundly with the rein he had untangled from his legs.

That was the least he could expect for such a dreadful offence as borrowing an expensive horse without permission. Addie was humbly thankful that no one told the Patron. Foreman Germaine would certainly have done so if he had thought it worth while. But as the Patron was so bewitched by these brats, he would probably just cut him short, as he had done over Mats.

"But if he goes and breaks the horse's leg or gets up to some mischief or other, you can be sure I'll get the blame," the foreman said bitterly as he thrashed Addie with the rein so that water flew out of his clothes.

"Get on off now, and just you say something about this if you dare," he said.

Addie didn't dare, because he was more frightened of the Patron than anyone else and anyhow he thought the ride had been worth the punishment. He wouldn't have been so angry with the foreman, if he hadn't been infected by Mats's hatred.

"That German!" he mumbled behind the foreman's back, just as the men did.

Otherwise, all was well with his life, and his friendship with Clio continued. When no one was looking and he was alone in the stable, he sat astride Clio's back in her box. It gave him a feeling that he was riding. His fat cheeks wobbled when Clio did her best to throw him. She hadn't forgotten the amusing game they had played and she liked having some fun, too.

In between, he helped the men with this and that, and when John could not endure the tasks of the spring slaughter, Addie took his place without complaining and whipped the blood at such a speed that the men were forced to praise him.

"Not like that there brother of yours," they said, when they asked him if he ever went to that garden John was always on about. But Addie was bold, refusing to be embarrassed on his brother's behalf. He just spat through the gap in his teeth.

"No, not me. I'd rather be in the stables," he said, cockily. The men laughed at the sight of his wobbling cheeks.

"Yes," they said. "Bet you wouldn't exchange blood pudding and pork for Christmas apples, would you now?"

"No, not me," said Addie loftily.

When the slaughtering was finished for the day, he went with the men into the kitchen for the extra meal laid on for the workers from now until Michaelmas, because the work then was more demanding than at any other time of the year. This meal was usually milk and waffles followed by a cup of coffee, and one of the maids stood all evening by the stove making the piles of delicious waffles.

But outside the kitchen, where at this time of the evening the sun warmed the ground, crofters, day-workers and the servant girls who did not eat at the manor squatted in a line, holding their meagre food-packs. They munched at cold potatoes and black coarse bread, enviously sniffing at the smell coming from the manor kitchen. They were pale and thin, craggy and bowed, easily distinguished from the manor staff, who were plump and red-cheeked, thanks to the good food of the manor.

Anna often walked past and saw them sitting there in the

meal-breaks. She always felt a stab in her heart at the sight of them. Although she had just been laughing happily at Sofia's antics in the sun, she was at once dispirited. She looked down at her fine new dress, the colour of it the same blue as the flowers in her hand, and at her shiny black patent-leather boots with their row of mother-of-pearl buttons. She remembered that there were children in the cottages who had never owned a pair of real shoes and whose clothes were so inadequate that they couldn't go out of doors all winter. She felt in debt to them in some way, because she had more than she needed, and they had less. It wasn't enough that she had kept her promise over the Karlberg children, that she had managed to help Mats Kari a little, or that she visited the poor now and again with a little food in a basket. That wasn't enough by a long chalk.

"Oh," she thought, sighing a little. "You can be as grand as anything in silk and velvet, everyone calling you Miss Anna, but inside you're nothing but Anna from Kulla, and the work is never done."

But despite her sighs she was pleased with what had already been achieved and the goodness the Patron had already shown. Rome was not built in a day was a phrase she had read in one of his books, and neither was there any magic formula which would at a stroke make everyone at the manor any happier.

"I'll have to take each day as it comes and do my best," she thought, trying to imagine the manor as a friendly oasis, where no one needed to starve to death like Mother Kari up in her cottage, or look as dispirited as the people squatting outside the kitchen.

It was easy to imagine that happy manor one day becoming

a reality, but beyond it lay a huge country of millions of people who had the same right to a good life. And outside that country, a whole wide world with even more millions of people in it, people of all kinds needing a helping hand and with just as much right to be happy as the people at the manor. Anna closed her eyes at the terrifying vastness of the thought.

"It's enough to take your breath away," she thought, feeling small and weak.

"Why are you looking so serious on this lovely sunny day?" said the Patron. He was sitting in a sunny corner of the veranda with a rug over his knees and was going through the mail the postman brought out twice a week.

"Come here, my dear," he added. "I've got some good news for you."

"Soffytina coming too," said Sofia, clambering up the veranda steps on all fours and thrusting a handful of flowers into his face. The Patron laughed and Pompi, who had been asleep at his feet, rose and blinked sleepily. Sofia selected two of the most crushed flowers and handed them to Pompi, who absent-mindedly ate them. The Patron laughed again and Sofia kissed him wetly on the chin.

"Soffytina's got a ganfie, just like Anna," she said again, very pleased with herself. Out of sheer contentment with the world, she extravagantly expended another flower on Pompi, but he had now woken up sufficiently to remember he was a dog, so he just sniffed and turned his back on her. Anna went to pick up Sofia, but the Patron waved her away.

"Let her be," he said. "It's all right, leave her."

He picked up one of the letters, put his monocle in his eye and read through it again. He looked pleased when he turned back to Anna.

"It's about Regina," he said. "She's allowed to come home at last."

There was a short silence and the Patron looked up at Anna.

"What is it, child?" he said. "Your face has gone quite white. Aren't you well?"

"Yes, I'm quite all right, thank you . . ." Anna pushed the curls away from her forehead and tried to smile.

"You've been out in the sun too much," the Patron said anxiously. "You must be more careful. You're still not quite strong. Sit down, child."

"Thank you," said Anna, sitting down on a chair, her knees quite weak. She ran her tongue round her lips and thought of saying something, but then changed her mind. The Patron looked down at the letter again.

"The doctors say Regina took the news that she would be a cripple for the rest of her life very badly. She is melancholy and bitter. She has to be distracted and amused as far as that is possible. That will be our task here at home."

"Yes," said Anna, straightening up, calm now, her eyes clear, her willingness to help and be useful overcoming the anxiety Regina's name always caused her.

"Yes, we must do everything we can for her," she said, promising herself that she would never for any reason whatsoever tell anyone about Regina's real intentions that day down by the ravine.

Thirteen

Regina came back to the manor.

They carried her in from the carriage and put her in a wheel-chair the Patron had sent for. She had become small and thin and her boyish back was crooked. Her face, with its long sharp nose, looked like a bird's, and was distorted by a scar that ran from one temple down her cheek. Her complexion was sallow, and against it, her black eyes looked like coals.

The servants had come out and were standing at a distance, curtseying to her in welcome. But she did not acknowledge their greeting. She turned to the Patron and said wearily:

"Send those gaping creatures away, Uncle dear. They torment me."

Anna had been standing beside the Patron, so she ran across and asked the maids to go in. It was easy to see that an injured person might well be hurt by curious gazes. But when she herself went over to greet Regina, Regina turned her head away impatiently.

"Leave me alone," she said. "Uncle, dear, I don't want to see any of your servants."

"But this is no maid," said Mr Sylvester in dismay. "This is Annemaria Beatrice Frederika, whom I found so miraculously. Don't you recognise her? You've met before. Mademoiselle told me."

"I don't remember, Uncle dear," said Regina, looking dutifully at Anna. "I should have known a maid wouldn't be wearing a velvet dress," she added. She wasn't looking at Anna, but at her dress.

"But you must be able to see the likeness!" cried the Patron. "Don't you see it's my dear daughter standing there." When they went into the drawing-room, where Mademoiselle had set out tea, he put Anna in front of the picture so that the light from the windows along the long wall fell on her hair, which was now down to her shoulders. Her curls shone like gold in the sun and her slanting dark-blue eyes, so like those of the girl in the picture, seemed even clearer than usual in the seriousness of the moment. Her complexion glowed rosily beneath the fair curls. The living girl was even more lovely than the girl in the picture.

"Don't you see? Don't you see?" said the Patron happily.

But Regina kept her eyes down, unwilling even to look. She was biting her lips to stop herself screaming with rage before this girl, so beautiful, while she was so frighteningly ugly and deformed. The girl would grow up, be happy and free, while she herself was chained to a wheel-chair and could only drag her martyred body across the floor with the help of crutches. When she thought about this same child being to blame for her own ruined life, her pain blended with a dark aching hatred.

The children had been told to come in and greet Regina after tea, but Regina did not wish to see them, either.

"Good gracious, Uncle," she said, with an expression of distaste. "Have you started up an orphanage? I've been longing to come back to the manor to get away from being in an institution. Is the whole house full of children?"

"Oh, no," said the Patron, embarrassed again. "There are only five of them. They're good, quiet children." He nodded encouragingly at the children, who were shyly hesitating in the doorway.

"Good gracious," said Regina again. "You seem to have become very fond of children in your old age, Uncle. You seem to have changed completely. How are you, by the way?"

"Me? Oh, I'm very well." The Patron glanced quickly at Regina through his monocle, not really sure what she meant. Then he looked hastily into the gilt-framed mirror on the wall. Did he look peculiar in any way?

Regina noticed his glance and suddenly smiled, an unpleasant smile which distorted her deformed face even more, her mouth twisting as if she could smile out of one corner of it only.

"Yes, you've changed, Uncle," she repeated. "Your face has become—how can I put it—kindly and—well, yes—a little childish, if you'll forgive the expression. One might almost think the childishness in the house had infected you. Don't be offended, Uncle, dear. But it's an amusing thought, isn't it?" Then she laughed again.

The Patron tried to laugh, too, but it was a very forced laugh and he at once turned serious again. He waved a trifle impatiently at the children.

"You can go," he said. "You can go now."

They all obeyed except for Sofia, bowing and curtseying

and stepping back. But Sofia came forward. She had been so occupied staring at the newcomer that she hadn't had time for her usual ceremonies. Now she came right in on tiptoe, her skirts swinging. She curtseyed to the bearskin, to the elk-head, to the old clock and the telephone, hesitating at the latter. Her eyes widened and her mouth fell open. The troll in the telephone . . . perhaps that was this strange person in the wheelchair? Had it escaped, the troll?

Sofia looked suspiciously at it, then raced across to the Patron, climbed up on to his lap and hid her face in his shirtfront.

"There now," said the Patron, suddenly embarrassed at what Regina might think. "There now, there now."

Anna hurried forward to take the child, but Sofia held on tight round the Patron's neck and it was impossible to shift her. She knew that if this was the telephone-troll, then the safest place was with the Patron He was the only person in the house who really knew how it worked.

"Soffytina be with Ganfie," she said, clinging on even harder. "Want be with Ganfie, want be with Ganfie." To strengthen her case, she kissed him again and again on his cheeks and chin and moustache.

Regina stared at them as if she could scarcely believe her eyes. A child in the Patron's arms! An ugly little crofter child sitting on her uncle's knee, and with approval . . . it was unheard of. Regina was suddenly filled with a fear in face of something she did not understand. Something had happened while she was away. A bunch of children led by that detestable fair-haired girl had invaded the manor, walked right into the great mansion house itself, into her uncle's mind, and changed everything. They had taken the place that had been Regina's and now she was excluded, ruined, and her life ahead nothing but an unbearable thought.

She suddenly covered her eyes with her clenched fists and cried out:

"I don't want to see them . . . those horrible . . . I don't want to see them. I cannot endure it."

She had cried out so loudly and hysterically, that the children scrambled over each other to get away, and the Patron himself had to take Sofia out, as she refused to let go of him. She did not calm down until they were in the pantry, where she allowed Anna to take her, and the Patron returned, pale and shaken, to Regina. The children crowded round Anna, looking up at her with unhappy eyes and pale faces.

"She didn't like us, Anna," they said. "She didn't like us."

"She's still got those evil eyes," whispered John. "She's still got those evil eyes."

Anna pressed her face against Sofia, whose whole body was stiff and rigid with fear, trying to hide her own unhappiness and sorrow.

"Yes," she whispered. "But we must all try to do our very best for her."

Fourteen

Winter seemed suddenly to have come back to the manor, cold and unpleasant indoors, silent and frozen and dead. The children were told to keep away, not to disturb anyone, not to show themselves more than necessary. In fact everything was as it had been in the beginning, as if spring had not managed to thaw the earth. Whenever the children happened to meet Regina in her wheel-chair on the ground floor, where the Patron had had all the steps removed, there was trouble. She complained that they disturbed her with their clumsiness, that they smelt of poverty and their appearance annoyed her.

"Keep them out of the way," the Patron said to Mademoiselle. "Keep them out of the way as far as possible. I can't have trouble in the house."

"They didn't cause trouble before, so they're not likely to now, either," protested Mademoiselle. "It'd be hard to find children as good and obedient as they are. So if there's trouble, then it will come from other quarters."

"Yes, I know," said the Patron impatiently. "But I want them out of the way all the same. Miss Regina can't stand them, and we must consider her and what she has been through."

"Yes," sighed Mademoiselle, as there was no answer to that. Of course you had to consider a sick person. She limped away; her bad foot had grown worse recently, and now she could hardly bear even a slipper on it. She went out to the kitchen and told the servants what the Patron had said and that they were to keep Sofia in the kitchen as much as possible. The others were old enough to obey of their own accord.

"You'll have to help me keep the child out of the drawing-room," she said. "We must see that she doesn't get in Miss Regina's way."

The maids all answered, "Yes, Mademoiselle," and "Certainly, Mademoiselle," but secretly they thought it a nuisance to be landed with a nursemaid's job on top of all their other work. But Agda went straight to the drawing-room, where Sofia was sitting neatly on the edge of a chair, turning the pages of an album with the very tips of her fingers, because she knew that when she was in there she had to behave herself. Agda grabbed her by the plaits and hauled her off the chair.

"That's the end of all this fine lady business now, you little creep," she said, pushing her out of the room.

But Sofia, thinking this was personal spite on Agda's part, bit the maid's hand sharply.

"Soffytina 'llowed here," she protested, pulling away. "Ganfie says Soffytina can be here."

"That's all finished now," said Agda triumphantly, pushing Sofia on towards the kitchen. "And stop biting, brat, or you hear from me, I warns you."

But Sofia struggled and twisted, and when she caught sight of the Patron through the study door, she at once started bawling.

"Ganfie! Ganfie! Ganfie, please come and say Soffytina can be here. Please come and say it."

But Regina was in the study too, sitting in her wheel-chair, her black eyes fastened on the Patron. Under her gaze, he was ashamed of his attachment to this crofter child. Gently, he closed the door so that he would not have to hear her cries. But Sofia's voice was shrill and penetrated through to him.

"Ganfie! Ganfie! Please, Ganfie, come and . . ."

"What is it the child calls you, Uncle?" said Regina. "Ganfie . . . what's that?"

"I don't know . . . I . . . I don't always understand her. She doesn't talk very well yet," said the Patron hastily, reddening like a schoolboy for letting a crofter child call him grandfather.

But Regina was thinking about the child climbing on to his lap and throwing her arms round his neck.

"With the best will in the world, Uncle," she said. "You'd better watch out that the child doesn't take too many liberties with you. You might lose the respect of the servants."

"Me?" said the Patron. "How can I lose their respect just because I show some kindness to these poor orphaned children? Aren't I allowed to show some mercy?"

Regina gazed out of the window and smiled her crooked smile.

"You've never shown any before," she said. "So people might think you're heading for a second childhood, as they say. It's easy to become a little . . . well, a bit foolish in one's old age. No, of course you're not, Uncle. But you know how people talk. Exaggerated kindness so easily seems foolish."

"What rubbish you talk," said the Patron angrily. "Rubbish, Regina!"

But from that day on, he put a stop to the children coming past the study to say good morning to him each day.

"Tell them to go straight to breakfast," he said to Anna. "I haven't time for them in the mornings now."

"But they'll be so miserable," protested Anna, thinking of Sofia most of all, who would not understand.

"The children can't rule the whole house," said the Patron. "Just see that they do as I say."

"Yes," said Anna, downcast.

The mornings that followed were difficult because, as Anna had feared, Sofia refused to understand why things had suddenly been changed. They had to carry her down the stairs and past the closed study door, behind which Regina was now having her coffee with the Patron. Otherwise they would not have been able to stop Sofia making her way in there by force. She cried and called out all the way, so in the end they had to put a hand over her mouth.

"Ganfie, Ganfie! Soffytina wants to say mornin'. Ganfie, please, Ganfie . . ."

It was a pitiful sound, and the Patron was so tormented by it that beads of sweat came out on his brow.

"I see that what Regina said is true. I've let them take too many liberties and now I'll have to suffer for it," he thought, wiping his brow.

But the weeping outside went on and could be heard through two doors. The Patron's coffee stuck in his throat, and he felt a sharp pain in his chest, as if his heart were bursting. Suddenly he opened the door and called for silence.

"Immediately!" he shouted. "Silence *immediately*." The cries ceased, and he knew that if they had continued he would have been forced to give in or die.

But the children were quite unaware of his thoughts. All they heard was his angry voice. They pushed Sofia into a corner and held a hand over her mouth until she was blue in the face.

"Anna!" they whispered in terror. "He's angry with us again. What shall we do, Anna?"

"If only I knew," said Anna, hanging on to the struggling, kicking, weeping child.

She was very confused, unable to fathom the source of the Patron's fury. Whenever Anna was present, Regina was always very careful about what she said, almost as if she were a little afraid of Anna, and she never looked straight at the girl. When she was forced to look at her, she always gazed at her dress, or her chin or her hair, and when she said anything, it was in a very low voice. She often asked very strange questions.

"I suppose you're pleased to see me sitting here like a . . . a cripple?" she said once, her black eyes fixed somewhere between Anna's chest and chin.

"How can you believe such a thing, Regina!" exclaimed Anna in dismay.

"Do you ever go out walking in the forest these days?" she asked another time. "Do you ever go up there by the ravine?"

"Sometimes, when I've an errand up at the crofts. If there's someone ill, or something," said Anna, calmly. "Then I might go that way. But otherwise I don't go walking in the forest, because neither Grandfather nor Mademoiselle like me to. And I haven't much time, either."

"They told me you suffered from loss of memory for a time," Regina went on. "How much do you remember of . . . of the time before?"

"Everything I need to remember," said Anna, trying to

catch Regina's eye. "If you just ask me, I'll give you an answer."

But Regina did not ask anything more.

Regina was cautious and rather frightened, because she didn't know how much Anna had understood of the events of the previous autumn, or what Karlberg might have let slip.

"What became of that idiot of a crofter living at Kulla before it was burnt down," she once asked the Patron. "Karlberg, his name was, wasn't it?"

"You mean the children's father?" he said. "He went to America and we've never heard from him since."

"I see," said Regina, so relieved that she had to smile.

"I remember now, of course," she went on. "He was the father of your charges, wasn't he? That accounts for it. Degenerate lot. They all look just as stupid as he did. Amazing that you've been able to stand having them in the house all this time."

"Oh, you get used to it," mumbled the Patron, unwilling to admit even to himself how quickly the stupid Karlberg children had managed to penetrate his heart.

"And you've done all this for Anna's sake, have you?" said Regina. "Really very handsome of you, Uncle."

"Anna's worth it, and more," said the Patron. When it came to Anna, the Patron did not have to hide what he felt, for no one would consider it foolish or childish to love your own kin.

"And more?" said Regina, smiling her crooked smile. "And more? Do you mean that labourer's boy, Mats? Anna helped him, too, I hear."

"Who told you that?" said the Patron. He wondered

whether Regina had heard about Mats spitting at him, too. He was angry both at the thought of someone telling Regina, and because she was smiling mockingly at him now.

"Who told you?" he repeated. "One of the servants? Tell me."

Regina pretended to think.

"I don't remember who it was," she said. "But it was one of the servants. They probably talk a lot more than you know, Uncle dear. They always do that when they start losing respect. Before that they simply dared not."

How cunning she was! She jabbed with pins wrapped in cotton-wool. No one knew until they felt the sting and then it was too late to ward it off. What use was it being angry with her later? The sting had touched and hurt, a constant reminder.

This matter of respect—the Patron could not meet the servants without asking himself whether they felt respect towards their master. Was there perhaps one of them being submissive to his face and mocking him behind his back, tittle-tattling about him, the Patron, becoming senile and childish?

The Patron grew suspicious and on his guard. He frowned at the men if they did not bow low enough, and if they bowed too low, he was angry about that, too, because then he thought they were ingratiating themselves. When the crofters came into his office to beg for a loan or credit, he refused them abruptly and showed them the door, because he never knew whether they had dared come because everyone said the Patron had grown so kindly in his old age that he was soft in the head. When he thought about all the things people might say or think behind his back, he was so annoyed that he almost countermanded the order he had given on seed-potatoes and demanded them back. Only the fact that the crofters had already planted them stopped him. He did not want people to say he had gone mad.

Fifteen

How well Regina knew her uncle! She knew how to deal with him and where all his weak spots were. She sat there in her wheel-chair, smiling her crooked smile, watching everything going according to her calculations. She saw the crofters and day-workers going round with anxious, frozen faces in the spring sunlight, and the labourers bowing and scraping, hardly knowing which leg to stand on to keep in with the Patron. She heard the foreman coming in with complaints about rebellious behaviour and laziness, asking permission to punish the men, and the Patron not raising a finger in objection.

"That's right. Maintain respect, that's all I demand," he said. And the foreman bowed his way out as respectfully as he reckoned the Patron would think suitable.

"Thank you, thank you, sir, thank you for your permission," he said. "I didn't wish to do anything against my master's wishes."

Then he went out and beat the labourer's boys, and shouted at them, and played at being master all day, excessively conscientious about everything. The men sighed and mumbled, but were forced to comply, for a steady paid job was not to be found on every bush at a time when people were hungry everywhere, with beggars standing along the roadsides, and orphaned children being put up for auction.

It was just the same indoors, for there Regina was really tightening the reins. She interfered with Mademoiselle's orders, changing them so that the maids didn't know what to think. If Mademoiselle said that the evening meal was to be crushed corn gruel with syrup, then Regina came in in her wheel-chair and gave orders for rye-flour gruel with whortleberries. If plates of smoked ham and pickled herring were brought to the Patron's table, Regina sent them out again, demanding smoked sausage and salted herring instead.

"The house shouldn't be run for the good of the servants," she said to the Patron. He had to agree, if only for the sake of respect.

But Mademoiselle had been in service for so many years that she had no intention of being pushed aside. She went on giving orders and deciding household matters as she had always done. So the maids, finding themselves with two mistresses, divided into two camps. One camp obeyed Mademoiselle and the other Miss Regina. There was constant strife between the two camps, and they also fought each other internally, telling tales on each other.

Mademoiselle went to the Patron, and complained. The Patron valued his housekeeper very highly, as she had always run his home with great thoroughness. So he promised to speak to Regina. But when he did so, Regina looked pityingly at him, apparently sorry for him.

"Such a lack of respect," she said. "Does even old Mademoiselle take such liberties that she complains to her master about a member of the family? Uncle, Uncle, don't let the servants treat you like this."

Although the Patron was offended and told Regina she was talking nonsense, he nevertheless thought a great deal about what she had said. The next time Mademoiselle came to see him about something that had gone wrong, he showed her the door with harsh words.

"Do you think I'm an old fool with nothing better to do than listen to women's chatter?" he said.

Regina, passing in her wheel-chair, heard what he said and saw Mademoiselle's shocked expression. She smiled maliciously. "Just as it should be," she thought. "Other people should taste what it feels like to be a bit unhappy." Only "a bit", because no one, no one could possibly be so unhappy as Regina herself.

It was remarkable how easy it was to create trouble and make people hostile and unfriendly to each other. The maids were all bad-tempered and snappy, Mademoiselle sullen and sighing at every other step she took, and the Patron kept himself to himself, walking round frowning, a suspicious look in his eye. The men were quiet when they came in for meals. They sat silently and sullenly, the older men bullying the younger ones, just as they were bullied by the foreman. It was just as Regina would have things, because it was not fair that she should be the only one to be unhappy.

In the middle of all this, Anna remained as friendly and helpful as before. She walked beside the children down the stairs in the mornings, after making sure as usual that they were washed and dressed properly. She joked and laughed with Sofia so that she would forget "Ganfie", who did not appear these days. She radiated motherliness and trust and calm. After the first few days of confusion and anxiety over the swift changes Regina's arrival had brought about, she had straightened up and thought about the children. It was no good looking helpless and perplexed in front of them. Then they would be completely lost and would not know what to do.

She did talk to John, as he was older than the others and understood more than most people thought.

"What shall we do?" she said. John answered according to the yardstick he always had in his mind.

"Let's stick to what you said before, Anna," he said. "Let's give of our hearts and do our best."

"Yes, let's do our best," repeated Anna, feeling strengthened. Although she was troubled by the Patron's curt manner and ruthless attitude, by Mademoiselle's sighs, the maids' bad temper and the strong words exchanged between the foreman and the men as a change from hostile and sullen silence, she kept her friendly gaze and deep down in her eyes, a smile was always lurking.

During the afternoons, she went with Sofia to fetch Addie from the stables and then they went to meet the other children coming home from school. It was spring now and the fields were full of flowers. There was frogspawn in great lumps in the ditches between the bright marsh marigolds. Steam rose from the marshes and the cuckoo called so loudly that it was almost out of breath.

They sat down for a while among the wood anemones, talking and laughing. They turned somersaults and walked on their hands and relaxed. Out here in the countryside, they disturbed no one, and no merciless eyes were watching their movements.

Sixteen

But Regina, sitting at the open window, heard their light voices and happy laughter in the distance and an aching bitterness seemed to fester inside her. She could not remember ever being allowed to laugh and play like that.

"No, never," she thought, remembering her childhood. She had grown up with Aunt Emily, a cousin of the Patron. Aunt Emily had taken it upon herself to take in young girls and give them an education and make them into young ladies. In her distinguished and formal home, loud laughter was forbidden and the very thought of a small girl turning a somersault would have made Aunt Emily stare with horror.

"And now, now it's too late. I can never again shout with joy, never move my body as I wish," thought Regina, striking her chest with her clenched fist, as if she were choking inside with bitter despair.

She picked up a little brass bell from the table and rang furiously for Agda, to whom it had fallen to wait on Miss Regina.

"Shut the window," she said sharply. "Shut the window."

But when she had calmed down, she realised that she was the only person she had shut inside. The ones she wanted to get, the children, went on playing happily outside in the sun.

She rolled her chair into the office, where the Patron was going through his papers. The window was open there, too, and the sound of children's voices and laughter came in from a distance. One voice was thinner and lighter than the others, squealing, making the Patron forget his papers and listen, a small smile appearing below his moustache. But when Regina's chair rolled in, he hastily stopped listening and returned to his papers.

"Uncle," said Regina. "It can't be good for those children to go rushing around and fooling about, making that noise all day."

"They don't," said the Patron, pretending to be in a great hurry with his papers. "They go to school, the older ones, I mean, and they have orders to help Mademoiselle and the maids and the farm men when necessary. That's Mademoiselle's responsibility. *I* haven't time to be a nursemaid," he added, taking the opportunity to hide behind his dignity, with which even Regina could not find fault now, so stern and inaccessible had he become.

But Regina was not to be put off.

"They don't need another nursemaid," she said, "Anna does that job." Then she burst out laughing.

"What strange times we live in," she went on. "Just think. Miss Anna Sylvester is a nursemaid and servant to a bunch of crofter brats. It really *is* ridiculous."

Mr Sylvester cleared his throat, twisted his moustache and rustled his papers.

"She's not their nursemaid," he said. "They're more like

brothers and sisters to her. I mean . . . that's what she thinks."

Regina stared at him as if what he had said was even more appalling.

"But, Uncle!" she exclaimed. "How *can* you let her think such a thing, to sink so low? She mustn't think of herself as sister to those brats. Her! A Miss Sylvester of a noble family."

The Patron tried to evade the issue.

"You know she promised to look after them," he said. "And a promise has to be kept."

"Anna's just a child," said Regina. "She doesn't have to be held responsible for what she happened to say a long time ago. It's bad for her to be with the children every day. It'll mean she'll continue to be a servant-girl to others, a little crofter girl. Just listen to the way she talks, Uncle dear. It's dreadful. You shouldn't really have those children in the house. Why don't you let the parish look after them again?"

Regina had overstepped the mark. The Patron sat up straight, looking very dignified.

"I have a promise to keep, too," he said. "Once I said, 'Come in, children, this is your home.' Those words were spoken. This is their home. They can stay here and grow up here until they can manage on their own. Anna has kept her promise throughout great difficulties, and nothing has been able to persuade her to break it or forget those little creatures. No, my dear Regina, *no*."

He looked at her gravely, twirling his moustaches. The corner of Regina's mouth fell. She was no longer smiling.

"How strange you've become, Uncle!" she exclaimed. "So completely unlike what you were before."

"Hm," said the Patron, rustling his papers, though keeping

his mouth firmly closed. He was prepared to keep his promise against all odds.

Regina thought for a while.

"Well then," she said. "Let the children stay, but send Anna away instead to learn manners and style. Send her to Aunt Emily for a while." As she said it, she smiled maliciously to herself, thinking of Aunt Emily's steely mind and formal, cold home. Anyone forced to live there for a few years would not find it so easy to sing and laugh and turn somersaults later. She knew that from her own experience.

"Aunt Emily would know how to turn Anna into a young lady," she said. "Aunt Emily is used to all sorts of young girls."

But Mr Sylvester fidgeted reluctantly. There was a lot of truth in what Regina had said. The neglect of Anna's education was a difficult problem that had to be solved in some way. But not this summer. The doctor had said she was to recuperate after her illness, and the Patron wanted to have her to himself at home as long as possible.

So he cleared his throat and remained firm.

"You know what the doctor said," he said to Regina. "Anna is to stay at home this summer. When the autumn comes, we'll see. We'll see."

At that moment they heard the sounds of the children approaching. The fresh spring breeze carried their voices with it. They were singing. Two pure clear voices kept the tune going, Anna's and John's, the others joining in now and again. Somewhere behind and alongside and ahead of the tune was another little voice, squealing and squeaking and piping and twittering and cooing at will. Regina suddenly saw the corners of the Patron's mouth twitching below his moustache, however hard he tried to suppress it, and his eyes turning mild below his stern brow.

She pressed her clenched fists against her heart and again felt the bitterness choking her inside. She could not bear those happy voices and she could not bear to see that the Patron, behind all his dignity and caution, was happy.

"I can't bear it," she thought. "I can't bear being the only unhappy one. I just can't bear it."

As she was unable to make them unhappy by separating them, she went on thinking up malicious comments on everything to do with the children and Anna. But chance began to play into her hands here, because strange things were happening at the manor.